MEET ME AT THE WILLOW TREE

SEQUEL TO "THE FEAR OF SOMEDAY"

BY JENNIE ENDICOTT

Dorrance Publishing Co
585 Alpha Drive
Pittsburgh, PA 15238
Visit our website at *www.dorrancebookstore.com*

ISBN: 979-8-89127-632-1
eISBN: 979-8-89127-130-2

Meet Me
at the
Willow Tree

Sequel to "The Fear of Someday"

Chapter 1

It's been eight months already since finding out that I was pregnant, an unplanned pregnancy I might add. Luckily for me my husband Mike is thrilled, and so is his entire family. I don't know what we would do without them. We had big dreams of moving to the beach at Pawleys Island, SC, where we first met, but that didn't happen. It couldn't happen.

My name is Jenna Graham Lewis, and my husband Mike and I are supposed to be in the Witness Protection Program, as well as his entire family. However, the Lewis family is a stubborn bunch and will not comply with the rules associated with being in witness protection. So, we live a quiet life at the cabin. For now, anyway. And well, we're not really all that quiet, but we stay out of public view as much as possible. We don't generally go out together as a family, because a large group would attract too much unwanted attention. Probably a smart decision. We're a bit of a rowdy bunch at times.

Mama is the one who made the tough call for all of us to go back to the family cabin after the capture of Lola and her father. While I absolutely love the cabin and all it represents, my heart was already won by the beach on my first visit. Or so I thought.

Additionally, Mama just feels like we're all safer in numbers. The cabin boasts plenty of rooms to accommodate a large family such as ours. And besides that, *no one runs me and my family from our home*, Mama had stated sternly, as if to be defiant.

The cabin has been in their family for many, many years, in fact for several generations. And we all know Mama wears the pants around here. What she says goes and that's just the way it is. I don't even mind. That woman earned my respect the day we met. And apparently no one else seems to mind taking direction from her either.

But for me, I'm just happy to be alive. I'm a survivor of many things to say the least. I'm pleased to say I've overcome a history of extreme fear as well as physical and emotional abuse imposed on me by my ex-husband James, the drug lord. But now I am living a new life with a family that I'm proud to call my own. The only fear I experience these days is about the upcoming birth of our daughter. I'm terrified, actually. I gave birth to mine and James's late son many years ago, so I know what labor is going to be like. A woman never forgets, trust me. Knowing that I'm going to deliver in less than a month has been weighing heavy on me lately. Not only because I don't like pain…of any kind, I don't want anyone associated with James to find out that I am having a baby. I still fear him even though he's dead. His reach is far, of this I am certain. There's no doubt he still has loyal members from his drug dealing cartel, including Lola.

Lola is his surviving love interest and a previous nanny to my son. Lola and her father, who are also drug dealers, are currently being held without bail, awaiting a trial date in the state of Texas, where I'm originally from.

At the time of Lola's capture, there was a supposed verbal agreement that Lola and her father's associates would leave us alone. They would stay out of our lives if we stayed out of their drug-dealing business. Meaning my husband Mike, who is with the FBI, and his brother Mac, who is with the DEA, would stop pursuing the take down of members associated with their cartel. Basically, they would turn the other cheek.

I know both sides well, and life experience tells me neither side will comply. Not in a million years. Mike and Mac will never be able to let them continue dealing drugs and living a life of crime for the sake of keeping the peace. And Lola will never let go of the grudge she holds for me. In her mind, I am the sole responsible person for the death of James, even though he was married to me at the time of his death. She was his girlfriend on the side. The next war is only a matter of time. I feel it.

I have, however, finally accepted that the drug world cannot be stopped, and people like Mike and Mac will always be on the hunt for the next big dealer. It's in their blood. While they say they're done chasing criminals, they both still talk about their jobs at the agency all the time. I know they miss it, but in all honesty, I wouldn't expect anything less from either of them. For them, it's like a game of cat and mouse, and there's always another mouse to catch. The rush they get from the capture, keeps them going. Animals hunting their prey in a way.

Both Mac and Mike made promises to Sonja and myself, that they were done playing the never-ending crime game and done with putting their lives in danger. Sonja is my sister-in-law and she is married to Mac, who is Mike's older brother. Neither of us believed them when they announced their retirement, but Sonja and I always hope the love for their family outweighs their love for law enforcement. Someone else can have a turn as far as I'm concerned. Just the thought of anything happening to either Mike or Mac can cause me to be an emotional wreck.

Throughout these last eight months, Sonja and I have become very close and for the first time in my life, I have a best friend. Someone I can talk to about anything and everything. I don't know how I ever survived life before having her. While I did have Mac as a dear friend, it's just not the same as a best girlfriend.

Sonja and Mac made it official after years of being on again and off again. She finally agreed to marry him if he gave up being a DEA agent. They were married after the apprehension of Lola and her dad, and right after Mac announced his official retirement. It was just a few weeks after that when Mike and I were also married. Sonja and I were each other's maid of honor. Even though we had small weddings, due to our current low-key situation, they were beautiful nonetheless.

After spending so much time with Sonja, we realized we had much more in common than just being married to brothers. We've both experienced abusive relationships and failed foster care childhoods. I think we have been crucial for each other's recovery.

Sonja is a few years older than me and several years younger than Mac. She's really quite beautiful, with her short, sassy hair. She flaunts a blond pixie cut, which is adorable on her but not everyone can pull off a cut like that. She has light brown eyes and flawless olive-toned skin. She's thin and very petite. She looks so tiny next to Mac. Her sassy personality matches her look perfectly. And she and Mac were made for each other, there's no denying that.

Prior to the takedown, she was a hairdresser. A big bonus for me! I had her freshen up my dark blond locks with a trim and light blond highlights just last week. I still wear my hair a little past my shoulders because I like the option of a bun or a loose ponytail. Especially these days, because of being pregnant, I'm just too tired some days to fix my hair. I'll be glad to get back to a normal size too. While I love being pregnant, I do not love feeling so big. I have a month to go, and I already can't tie my own shoes. Mike still tells me I'm beautiful every day without fail and I love and appreciate that about him. He still makes me feel so special.

Speaking of Mike, I just heard him come in.

"Hey, babe," he hollered from the kitchen.

"Hi," I replied, walking to greet him with a kiss. "I was just wondering what you were up to today."

"Not much, hanging with Mac," he replied. "You know, doing guy things." He laughed and then leaned down to kiss my belly.

"Really? Guy things? You mean working on cars again," I said.

He looked at me with some version of guilt showing in his beautiful eyes before he responded.

"What's wrong with working on cars? I like cars. In fact, I love the smell of the exhaust. I love the roar of a Hemi. I like having greasy hands and clothes. Real men love cars. You know you're one of the lucky ones to get such a manly man. I think I'm a great catch…just saying." He started laughing at himself yet again.

"Am I now?" I asked.

"You definitely are," he confirmed proudly. That earned him an eyeroll and a head shake.

"Next subject," I said. "I'm going to take a nap, but where is Dune? I feel better when he sleeps with me." Dune is our adorable blond, misbehaved rescue puppy.

"He's outside with the other puppies," Mike advised. "Do you want me to get him for you?"

"Yes, please. I need him when I nap," I said again with a big smile.

He paused briefly and then asked me if he had been replaced by a puppy.

I simply grinned and then responded by telling him, "It could happen. You just never know. Why? Are you a little jealous?"

"Actually, I'm a lot jealous," he said, almost serious. "But I'll go get him for you, anyway," as he turned to walk away.

"After you bring him to me, you can get back to doing those important manly things," I teased. I got a hand wave in response. I almost think he's happy that I'm going to go nap. Not sure how I feel about that, I was thinking as I crawled into my bed. But I didn't think about it long. Sleep came fast. I didn't even hear him come in to put Dune in bed with me.

CHAPTER TWO

I woke up a few hours later, thinking about my son Junior again. I just wish things could have been different with him. Junior was born when I was just sixteen. Unfortunately, he made some poor life choices and ended up being shot in a drug raid. He fired first on law enforcement, causing them to fire back. Those shots resulted in his death. A part of me will forever grieve for him. Although the ache is more bearable than it once was. I guess time does mostly heal your wounds, no matter how deep they are.

Even now with his father James dead and buried, this case of capturing a drug lord and his family has proven to be dangerous. So dangerous, we'll all most likely be looking over our shoulders for the rest of our lives. I knew he would haunt me from his grave. "Bastard," I mumbled under my breath.

While we now live with watchful eyes and a lack of trust for almost everyone outside our family circle, we do all still seem to enjoy being together, so that's a bonus. We are currently all living together at the family cabin while we await the trials for Lola, her father, and several of James's men. I believe this family could withstand just about anything. And, actually, we've already survived a lot.

As I was still lying in bed, having all these thoughts, Dune pounced on me and I started laughing at him. My mouth must have been wide open at the right moment because the next thing I knew, he gave me a big, wet, slobbery kiss right on my teeth! Yuck! While I'm thankful for this cute little guy, I could do without those kinds of kisses. A lick on the cheek would suit me much better. *I mean, he licks his parts,* I was thinking to myself. That's just… Eeeew

Out of the five puppies our family members took from the litter found on the island, I ended up with the wildest one of all. *Why is that?* I wondered. Although I should have expected it, since Mike picked him. He would pick the rowdy one. The thought of Mike brought a smile to my face. *I think I'll head outside to see what they're doing.*

On my way out, I grabbed an apple from the basket on the kitchen table and headed out to the tunnel. That's where Mike and Mac generally work on their cars. Honestly, as much time as they spend out there supposedly working on cars, I can't understand how there is anything left to fix. By now, their cars should be in perfect working order, and if they're not, I'd say they need to hire a real mechanic.

It's a beautiful walk to the tunnel. Honestly, it's beautiful no matter where you walk to on this property. The streams, the river, and the rolling hills are breathtaking. It feels so pure and untouched. Not too far past the tunnel entrance, I can see the willow tree in the near distance.

Unfortunately, Mike and I haven't been back to the cottage or the willow tree. I'm just not ready. I'm still afraid James's ghost is there waiting on me. Silly, I know, but I'm just being honest with myself. Mama shot and killed James at the cottage in order to save me from his last brutal attack.

I approached the tunnel and could hear Mike and Mac talking with someone. A voice that sounded familiar. I stopped for a moment to rest and to also try and hear what they were talking about.

This is wrong to eavesdrop, I thought, but the words I heard were crystal clear. There was no misunderstanding. Lola had escaped from prison, and they were going to assist with the case. I knew it! My legs instantly felt like well-done noodles. It's been a while since I have cried but there they were, tears and lots of them. No stopping the river of emotions pouring out of me this time.

How could this be possible? I can't wrap my mind around the words I just heard, and there's no mistaking what I heard.

I managed to get the rest of the way to the tunnel opening. "Oh, hey, babe," Mike said, looking up from whatever they were looking at.

I didn't greet them with a warm, pleasant tone like normal. Instead, I replied with, "I heard you talking. I heard all of you. You promised you were done with the DEA, Mac. Same for you," I said, turning to Mike. "You said you were done with the FBI. How is it even possible for Lola to escape a maximum-security prison? I hope someone has a very good explanation for that." More tears came pouring. "How do you know she's not here somewhere already? She could be lurking outside right now, watching all of us. The thought of that is not comforting.

How long ago did she escape and when did you plan on telling your wife?" So many questions right now. I finally stopped talking to give one of them a chance to respond.

I felt weak. Mike just looked at me as if he were at a loss for words and stood there with a blank stare, completely speechless. Mike is never without words; he always has a witty comeback. But not this time. Mac started speaking first. "I'm sorry, Jenna. We just found out ourselves when Jimmy called last night."

"Last night? You didn't think to mention it to your wife?" I asked, turning to look at Mike.

"Jenna, we weren't keeping it from you," Mac continued. "We were just trying to decide the best course of action before telling everyone. You're pregnant, and we didn't think you needed the added stress."

"That wasn't your call to make. We are talking about my life too.

"Does Mama know?" I asked.

"She does," Mike replied, "and so does Pops."

"Oh my god… I can't believe this is happening, again," almost in hysteria. "I told you she would keep coming for me. What about our baby? How will she ever be safe?" I could see Jimmy watching me. I looked at him and told him not to get any ideas or I'd kick him in the balls.

"Yes, ma'am," he replied, taking a step back.

Last time I had a meltdown he gave me a shot that knocked me out for hours. He said it was justified because I was having a meltdown on the helicopter. While he is a certified paramedic, and I was technically freaking out, that did not give him the right to take it upon himself to "medically treat" me. At least in my opinion.

Turning back to Mac and Mike, "What happens now?" I asked.

"We may need Jimmy's help once again, to move us to another secure location," Mike replied.

"There is no safe secure location," I said, rather snide. "Every time we move, they find us." Everyone became silent. I'm guessing because they knew I was right.

Mike came to hold me, and I let him. "I just don't have the strength to do this again. I just don't. Take me back to the house," I asked, actually more like pleading. He didn't say anything, but I could see the worry on his face. He helped me up in his truck and then he went back to the driver's side and hopped in. We were silent. I was mad.

Once we arrived back at the cabin, I went to our room and quite aggressively shut the door. Mike was right behind me but all he got was a door slam to the face. I didn't even care in that moment. I hollered out to him, "No need to send your mama to talk to me either. It won't work this time." Mike didn't respond. I guessed he went on his way already on account of my anger. But that's okay. I need a moment to think anyway.

•　　•　　•　　•　　•

After a few minutes of crying, I was calm, but I am still way beyond upset. Why do men think they can sneak around, pretending to work on cars, all the while hiding something as big as this? We should have gone into Witness Protection when it was offered, but no, we have stubborn-ass men who think they can handle it all on their own. Take down an entire drug ring alone. Well, they can't. It's not even reasonable for them to think they can. I sat on my bed for a short time pondering all of this until I became even more angry.

A few minutes later, I opened my door only to find Mike still standing there. Apparently waiting on me. "Does Sonja know about this?" I asked him. "How about Kristy?"

"No," he softly replied, almost as if he regretted his decision to not tell me.

"Well, they're gonna know now. This family does not keep secrets, at least that's what you led me to believe. I'm a fool for trusting any of you. I'm going to tell them all right now," as I headed out the bedroom door towards the family room.

"Jenna, stop. Let's talk about this," he pleaded.

"No thank you," I retorted in a sarcastic tone. "I'm done talking to you."

I found Kristy first and just let my mouth take over. Attitude and all. "Did you know that Lola escaped from prison?" I asked her.

"Oh no," she replied in a panicked voice. "Where are Ava and Ana?"

"I don't know," I told her, "but I would find them right now and keep them close if I were you." Right then Sonja was coming to see what was going on. I didn't have to say anything because Kristy was already delivering the grim news to everyone else. One by one, the rest of the family became aware of Lola's escape because of the panic I created.

"There…now the whole family knows," I said.

Ummm… I may have just caused a situation of panic. Maybe that wasn't the right thing to do, but I think it's very inappropriate that we all didn't know immediately about Lola's escape. Everyone could be in danger if she's close by and lurking around. Family first, right?

I turned and went back to my room, scooping up Dune on the way. If I had a sign that read "No Visitors," I'd hang it on the door. I just wanted to be left alone. I crawled back into bed and once again fell asleep. Being pregnant is exhausting.

Chapter Three

When I woke a few hours later, I headed towards the kitchen. The entire family was all gathered around the table, discussing the impending Lola situation. No one else seemed to be angry. So why was I so mad? I could see them together like always, acting like nothing was wrong, laughing and snacking. It hit a nerve with me this time for some reason. This was the first time since meeting all of them that I could honestly say I felt like an outsider. I felt like I didn't belong there, a crushing blow to my heart. My eyes began to fill with tears as I watched them.

Just then Dune came running past me like the tornado he is and ran straight to Mike in the kitchen. Mike picked him up. Dune is one of seven rescue puppies, and probably the worst behaved. Dune is adorably mischievous. That's the best way I can describe him. He gets into everything. He wants to play nonstop and is somewhat defiant if he doesn't get his way. He talks back in a dog sort of way, so you can't even be mad at him when he looks at you with his big brown eyes. Gets me every time.

I turned to walk away, hoping no one saw me. Unfortunately, Dune's shenanigans got Mike's attention and I knew he saw me. He got up to follow me to our bedroom. Mike closed the door behind him. He hugged me and he told me he was sorry and that he was planning to tell me about Lola's escape. He further explained that he really had been working on cars with Mac and only knew about Lola's escape because of Jimmy. Jimmy wanted us to have a heads up before anything bad happened. Jimmy is Mac's longtime friend and who Mac calls when the family needs protection.

I apologized to him for maybe overreacting just a little, but that I felt a family meeting should have been called right away. "We have a daughter on the way, and our first priority as her parents is to protect her. She certainly didn't sign up for any of this."

"I agree, and I'm really sorry. I am protecting all of us, and our daughter will always be a priority. Don't ever doubt that."

"Are you going back to the FBI?" I asked.

"I don't know," he said. "I'm sorry, I know that's not the answer you're looking for. It's just that sometimes I feel like I left without taking care of business. Like it's unfinished, and I didn't give it everything I had. That's not who I am. You should understand that more than anyone. You lost your son. Someone else could lose their son or daughter if we don't stop them." Then he got quiet.

I did, too, but only for a moment. "I'm sure you see the sadness in me quite often over the loss of Junior, and I'm sorry for that, but it's not your fault, it's not my fault. I don't blame you but somehow you blame yourself. And you shouldn't.

"But…" I continued, "broken promises are no good either. The only thing I need right now is for you to be honest. If you're considering going back to the FBI, then just say it. Please don't treat me like a delicate flower because I'm pregnant or because of my past. That's all I'm asking for from you."

We sat on the bed and just held each other. I whispered, "I'm strong and have never felt better."

He replied by softly saying, "I know you are. I just worry about you," squeezing me a little tighter.

After a few minutes passed, Mike asked me if I was ready to go to the kitchen with the rest of the family. I wasn't really feeling like being around all of them at the moment, but I agreed to go anyway.

I was quiet throughout most of dinner, and I didn't eat much. While the last eight months had been absolutely perfect, I feared the path we were currently on would only lead to nothing good. Worry had once again set in, stealing the final joys of my pregnancy. I didn't even know where I'd be when she's born. *How am I going to find a new doctor in the last month of my pregnancy? It's absurd to be even thinking about this right now. I'm not supposed to be traveling this late in my pregnancy either. I'm sure no one is thinking about me being pregnant and close to giving birth.*

I could feel Mama watching me but I never met her eyes. I'm sure my own eyes were showing more than I wanted them to. *I'll be back to riding the train of despair until this next chapter is over. So much for getting the fairy tale. It was short lived.*

I excused myself from the table, grabbed my bag, and went outside for a walk. Alone…and no one followed. My mood must be radiating the "keep away, I bite" signals and I'm okay with that for now. This misery does not love company.

I turned and headed towards the willow tree. I don't know why. I often think about that magnificent tree where Mike and I made love for the first time. It was so special, magical, really. If I close my eyes, I can remember the passion, the urgent need for him to be mine. It was the same for him. Mike and I are convinced our daughter was conceived on that beautiful afternoon. So convinced, we decided to name her "Willow Grace" after it. It will forever be a special place for the both of us. I just want to feel that way again, even if only for a moment. Lately, it just seems so hectic.

I spread the vines apart and went in. For a brief time, I was scared of being alone, unprotected by Mike and Mac. That old, vulnerable feeling had returned. I decided to stay and work through my fears. I reached into my bag and pulled out the journal Mama had bought for our baby girl and my black pen. My first entry in the journal would be about today. I'll share with her, all of the details from today's events. I pulled a small, short branch from the tree and placed it in my bag. I'll dry it out and then securely place it on today's journal page when I get home. Our daughter should know the journey of her parents. I can only pray that we capture Lola once more. As far as I know, her dad is still securely locked away. I'll keep my fingers crossed that it stays that way.

Several hours have passed and it's starting to get dark. I came out from under the tree and headed back to the cabin.

Feeling a little spooked with Lola on the loose, I picked up the pace. The thought of me making a poor decision to leave the cabin was heavy on my mind. Faster, faster, faster…

Once I was in a close proximity to the cabin, I could see all of them in the living room watching television, so I felt like I could now slow my pace. Mama had finally broken down and allowed a television at the cabin. But only because we are all living there for now. Mama didn't allow televisions at the cabin before because it was supposed to be the place for sacred family time.

I didn't see Mike with them. *Hmmmm… Wonder what he's up to now?* I bypassed everyone and went straight to my room to shower. Mike was waiting for me.

"Hey," he said to me in a sad, pitiful voice.

"Hey," I said back to him.

"Are you still mad?" he asked.

"I'm not mad, Mike. I'm disappointed, and I'm scared."

"I know you are and I'm sorry," he said. "If it makes you feel any better, we unanimously decided we're going to wait it out here at the cabin, to see if Lola or any of her men come back to our location. Mac and I know we can't do this alone. Jimmy's agents will arrive in the morning. They can sleep in the sunroom."

Another decision made without me. Interesting, I thought to myself. *It wasn't that unanimous.* But I kept my thoughts to myself.

"Mac and I are both going to assist with the apprehension of Lola. Then, I promise, we're done for good. We're only assisting with the case, not running the show so to speak."

"Don't make promises you can't keep," I said.

"How did Sonja take the news?" I asked.

"About like you did," he said. "She's pissed. I haven't seen her since Mac told her."

I got up to go look for her, but Mike asked me to please stay with him until we've talked this out. "I hate seeing you so upset and unhappy," he said.

"I'm okay, Mike. Really, I am. I'm glad we're staying at the cabin. But just to clarify, we're still good to have our baby at the hospital, right?"

"About that," he said. Then his whole look changed.

He's about to drop a bomb, I know it with every breath of me.

"What now?" I said, getting more annoyed by the second.

My hormones are out of control. I do not recognize myself at all right now. This no-patience, irritable, feisty thing I have going on may be a bit much. I'm making my own self tired. Is that possible? I can't imagine how everyone else is feeling being around me.

My thoughts quickly shifted back to Mike. I was still standing, looking down at him.

"Well, Mama has a thought," he blurted. "Just hear me out."

"This cannot be good—" I started to say, but then there was a light knock at the door. It was Mama. I let her in. Still annoyed and looking at the both of them, I had no words. They obviously hatched some ridiculous plan about the birth of my baby without me.

Mama started to speak. She asked Mike to leave so that she and I could have a moment. He told Mama he wasn't sure if that was a good idea. She told him it'll be fine and pulled the door open a little more so he could exit the room. He did as she asked, like always. Mama shut the door behind him and asked me to have a seat on the bed. After I sat, still looking at her, she sat down beside me and began to speak.

"I'm sorry if things aren't going as planned, but things rarely do. It's up to us to make the best of whatever situation we have been presented with. I know this should be a joyous time for you and, again, I'm sorry it's not.

"Please don't be too hard on Mike and Mac for having your best interest at heart. You have been all that either of them has thought about since they first met you. And both of them have adjusted their entire life around you for the last year at least, if not longer. We all have."

In that moment the guilt I was feeling was like carrying a boulder. The weight was relentless, and I was suffocating. I started to tear up, because I knew that she was right. I've been the selfish one. "I am so sorry," I said, almost feeling embarrassed about my behavior.

"I'm not done," she said and continued speaking. "If you're okay with it, I'm going to deliver your baby. I'm a retired nurse, as you know, and Jimmy is a paramedic who will be there on standby. I do have labor and delivery experience and I'm certain not much has changed about giving birth. This will keep the birth out of the paper, so that no one knows until we're ready to share your news.

"Your pregnancy has been without complications, and your ultrasound last week was normal. There is no reason this plan can't work," Mama said. "At the end of the day, we'll all be safer, including your baby girl."

I looked at her in utter shock, horror, and disbelief. *Did I hear all of that correctly? They want me to have a home delivery.*

What are they thinking? I just don't know what to say, and I certainly don't think I want a home delivery. How can that be safe? What if something goes wrong?

Ridiculous or genius? The jury is still out. I have a lot to think about.

I halfheartedly hugged her and said, "I need time to process all of this. I appreciate your need to protect everyone. Can we talk about this further in the morning?"

"Of course we can," Mama said. "I love you," she added. "Now get some rest," she said sternly. She walked out, closing the door behind her, leaving my mind in a whirlwind of thoughts.

She's a retired nurse. Why does this seem so scary? And not to mention wrong on so many levels.

I know she's trying to be retired, but her two sons keep her on her toes. Instead of going to the hospital every time one of them gets shot, they call their mama. Mac and Mike say it comes with the job. I, personally, think it's crazy. With today's medical capabilities, why would you call your mama when you get shot, instead of going to a hospital?

Now she's going to be a labor and delivery nurse? I don't know that I'm in agreement but nevertheless, I'm thankful for her every day. I am literally alive because of her. Had she not showed up with a shotgun when she did, it's hard to say what would have happened on that awful day at the cottage. I really don't like to think about it, but I do from time to time anyway. It's hard not to, but I will forever see the image in my mind of her taking the fatal shot that ended James's life. And now she'll be the one to bring a new life into the world. Poetic justice maybe?

I just don't know about any of this. I'm going to sleep on it. Obviously, this has already been discussed with Mike and who knows who else. Certainly not with me until now. Trying to move past my angry self as I'm thinking about the words Mama had for me earlier. I know she's right about Mac and Mike having my best interest at heart, and I know what they have sacrificed for me.

So much to process. What I need is a trip back to the beach. I'm starting to feel like I'm losing myself all over again. I'm overwhelmed. I started to cry but quickly pulled myself together.

CHAPTER FOUR

I tried to sleep but I'm feeling unsettled. I feel like there's a giant storm cloud following me. Then suddenly I remembered Sonja is upset too. I was on my way to see her earlier when Mike and Mama kind of ambushed me. She has good reason to be upset too. Mac promised her he was going to retire. That's the only reason she agreed to marry him in the first place and the same reason why they weren't married long ago. I need to find her. I'm getting that feeling again that something is not right.

I left my room and went to the kitchen. Mama and Pops were sitting at the table, drinking an iced tea. "Have you seen Sonja lately?" I asked. "Mike said he hasn't seen her all day."

They both said they hadn't seen her.

"I'm getting worried," I told them. "I can't imagine where she could be." I turned to walk away and remembered we all have burner phones. I haven't really needed a phone since being at the cabin, but I'll grab mine from my room and give her a call.

I was calling her, but no answer. There's no way she would leave without telling me. She just wouldn't. I called again and could hear her phone ringing, so I followed the sound. Once more it went to voicemail. I called a third time. This time I found her phone laying on the back porch. Panic has set in yet again.

I went back to the kitchen to tell Mama I had found Sonja's phone. Then I asked her if she knew where Mac might be.

Right then Mac and Mike walked into the kitchen. Mike announced, "There's no need to worry because she already left. I told you she was angry with Mac. Apparently, she's really angry."

"I can't believe she didn't tell me. I'm so sorry, Mac. Why wouldn't she take her phone though? That just doesn't make sense."

We were all in agreement that it didn't seem right. "Are you sure she left? Maybe she's at the river or in the tunnel," I said.

"Trust me, I checked everywhere," Mac said.

Mike asked me for her phone. "Maybe she called someone we don't know about yet," he said, scrolling through her call history. The history confirmed she made three calls to the same number. He hit redial and found that her calls were made to the beauty shop where she worked prior to all this madness.

Both girls, Ana and Ava, walked in just then and asked for a snack.

"Of course. I'll get you something." While making them a snack, I asked if either of them had seen Sonja. They both said they had in fact seen her earlier walking towards the long driveway with a bag. They just thought since everyone else is acting mad today, that she was going for a walk because she was mad too. Ana said it didn't seem like something they needed to mention to anyone. I thanked both girls for telling us and sent them on their way with their snacks in hand.

I turned back to Mac and told him, "I'm not even sure what to do with this information."

"I'm going to drive down to the end of the driveway," Mac said. "Maybe she's still walking. I have no idea which direction she would go if she did make the five-mile trek to the end of the driveway."

"I'm going with you," Mike said.

"Me too," I added.

We headed towards the tunnel to get his car. The tunnel is pretty long. It runs from the back side of the house, behind the tree line to just before the willow tree. Mama believes the willow tree was planted there as a marker for the tunnel. The tree is obviously very old, and so is the cabin. The tunnel would not be easy to find if you didn't know about it. *If only walls could talk*, I thought. Imagine the history in this house and on this land.

My mind went to the cottage where James was killed. I guess that officially made him part of the history here. I found that to be both disturbing and sad. I need to think about something else before I cry again. Somehow, he seems to be able to taint every part of my life.

After driving the five miles and reaching the entrance to the property, there was no sign of Sonja but there was a fresh set of tire prints. Someone definitely picked her up. But who, is the question.

As we were driving, my phone rang. I didn't recognize the number but answered it anyway. It was Sonja and she was in a state of panic. I could barely understand what she was saying. I asked her to calm down, but she only became more upset as she spoke. She said, "They are being chased by a black SUV."

"Sonja, where are you and who are you with?"

She replied with the name Susan, adding that she doesn't know where she is.

Mac grabbed the phone from my hand and put her on speaker, so we could all hear. "Sonja, are you okay?" he asked her. "What direction are you going?"

She replied by telling Mac she was sorry. There were shots fired, tires squealed, and then nothing. Silence. We all just looked at each other in shock.

"What the hell just happened?" Mac asked after a brief moment.

Mac looked like he was going to cry but didn't. He immediately took charge by calling Jimmy to tell him what had happened. Jimmy said he would round up the crew and head to the cabin.

"Listen, Mac, all of you need to get back here," Jimmy said.

"I can't," Mac replied. "I have to find her."

"I agree," Mike said, "but we need to take Jenna back to the cabin first, and then we can go back and continue looking." Mac agreed to taking me back and turned around.

I just sat there in the car, feeling helpless. I couldn't stop worrying if Sonja was okay. And who was Susan? I think it's safe to assume she's someone from the beauty shop because that's where her last calls were made to. I'm still puzzled and maybe a little hurt that Sonja didn't tell me she was leaving. And now, I can only pray that she's okay.

They dropped me in front of the cabin and watched me go in before turning to leave. I found the family all together in the living room. Jimmy and his men had weapons drawn. They had a man posted on all perimeters of the house. It looked like a scene straight out of a scary movie. In no time, I felt like I was reliving the escape from the mansion I shared with James and Lola. I was trembling. I took a seat in the big, double round chair. It's Mike and I's favorite place to sit and cuddle.

Kristy obviously could see that I was visibly shaken and came to sit with me by the enormous stone fireplace. I hugged her and thanked her as we held each other. Mark, who is Kristy's husband, stayed with Ava and Ana on the couch. Mama and Pops sat in their respective recliners. No one knew what to say. We all just sat there looking at each other. And just like the last attack on this family, I blame myself. I just can't help it. Their life was probably event free until they met me. I didn't cry but I wanted to.

Chapter Five

About an hour had passed, and while sitting there, my back started hurting. Not bad at first but more like this intense pressure. I felt like I had to pee. Oh, a sharp pain, enough to cause a wince. A few minutes later, another one. "I'm pretty sure I'm starting to have contractions," I told Kristy. "No…no…no… This can't be happening," I said out loud. "I'm almost a month early." I squeezed Kristy's hand. "Oh my god, it hurts."

"Mama!" Kristy hollered. "I think the baby is coming."

Mama rushed over to me. "I think this is it," I said. "I'm not ready. Where's Mike? I can't do this by myself." I cried in pain as the next contraction came. I started to feel like I couldn't breathe. I'm terrified. In that moment I was thinking to myself that anyone who would do this a second time clearly had no brains. Right now, I fall into that category.

Mama held my hand as she helped me up. I felt the gush of warm, wet liquid running down my legs and soaking my pants. My water has definitely broke. Even if I decided to go to the hospital, we're a little late. It's more than an hour from the cabin. I was shaking uncontrollably. This is really it, without a doubt. Willow Grace is on the way whether we like it or not. The timing could not be worse. She and I will have a discussion one day about the additional drama and stress she caused today. It did make me smile at the thought of that, but it was short lived. The next contraction came, and it was much worse than the one before. "I can't do this," I cried to Mama.

"Oh honey, we're a little past that," she said. "You have no choice now, but it's going to be okay. I promise," she said.

I just cried.

Mama led me to the room where she removed the bullets in the past from Mike and Mac. This room looks like a mad scientist lives here. What in the hell was I thinking when I agreed to such a primitive delivery. Oh wait…I didn't officially agree. This is barbaric to say the least.

Mama hollered for Kristy to bring lots of towels and hot water as she helped me climb up on the table. I nearly passed out as all of this was happening. "No, no," Mama said. "Stay with me. We have a baby to deliver."

"Where's Mike?" is all I kept saying.

"He'll be here as soon as he can be," Mama said.

Mama is still so calm. I don't know how but she is. She pulled off my soaked pants and underwear and tossed them to the side. All the sudden I was seriously concerned and embarrassed about my mother-in-law seeing my vagina. She can't unsee that. Oh Lord, this is the most horrific day of my life, when it should be the best. She'll always look at me and see my vagina. I cried harder. Another contraction came.

From there it's all a blur. Next thing I know, Mama handed me our perfect little girl. "Mike missed it all," I told Mama.

"No, I'm here," he said. I looked up and sure enough, he was here standing behind me out of Mama's way. Somehow I never heard him come in. He walked over to my side and picked up our daughter. He was in awe. "Look what we did, Jenna. She's beautiful." I cried, but only because everyone is so happy, including me.

I thanked Mama for being here and bringing Willow Grace safely into the world. She kissed my forehead and smiled but said nothing. I guess that's her way of saying you're welcome.

After the initial excitement and things sort of calmed down, I remembered that Sonja is still missing. "Is there any word on Sonja?" I asked.

"Not yet," Mike said, adding that Mac left again to go look for her. Jimmy was going to go with him but Mama said he needed to stay since he's a paramedic. Just in case something went wrong with the delivery. Luckily everything went smoothly.

"I'll let him know he's free to go," Mike said.

Mama then said, "Let's get Jenna and the baby up to your room so she can rest and work on feeding her."

Mike helped me put on a big, warm nightgown after a very quick shower. I feel a bit cold and weak but that's normal, if I remember correctly. I'm so tired. I crawled into bed after we put Willow in her crib. Mike said he would stay with her so I could sleep, and sleep I did.

I woke up about six hours later. Mike was holding her. "I can't stop looking at her," he said to me.

"I know. She's so perfect," I said proudly.

"Jenna, I love you so much, and I love our daughter more than you can even imagine. I promise to protect both of you. Please trust me."

"I love you too, Mike, and I do trust you." He walked over and kissed me softly on my lips. Then he sat beside me and handed Willow to me.

"She's so tiny and perfect," he said.

"I'm glad you didn't miss it, Mike."

"Me too. I wouldn't have got to hear you freaking out about Mama seeing your vagina. You were funny when you weren't mad."

"Oh no, I remember thinking that, but I can't believe I actually said it out loud. I bet your mama thinks I'm mentally unstable."

"No, she doesn't," he laughed. "She said it was the pain talking."

"Ugh," was all I could say.

"Has anyone changed her diaper since I was asleep?"

"Yes, I took her to Mama for a quick tutorial. I'm not going to lie, I was terrified. She just seems so small and fragile. Mama said she only weighs five pounds and three ounces. And besides, she pooped. I can't do poop diapers." He laughed at himself.

All I could do was just look at him. She's been here less than eight hours and he's already decided he "can't" change poop diapers. He took her to his mama. Why am I not surprised? Then I laughed too. He is so charming, and I am so in love with him. How can I be mad at him? He is by far the most amazing person I know.

Just then, there was a light knock on the door. "Come in," I hollered. It was Kristy the girls Ava and Ana. Next thing

I knew, everyone was there to see the baby, except Mac and Sonja. I was sad they missed it. Sonja was so excited about us having a baby but left before she was born. I'm sure she has a very good reason. I just pray she's okay and that Mac finds her…soon. I'm so worried.

Mike asked me if I would mind if he went to look for her too. He said, "Mama would love to stay with you for a while, if you're okay with it."

"I'm perfectly okay with it. We have no secrets now," I said lightheartedly.

Everyone laughed, including Mama.

Chapter Six

Kristy and Mama helped all night with Willow. She cried several times for a bottle and diaper change, and they were quick to respond. I just rolled over and went back to sleep. The next morning, I actually felt pretty good. "I want to get out of bed," I told Mama. She helped me to the shower and then to the kitchen. I was starving. "I would love some pancakes, Mama." She was happy to make them for everyone. It was a much-needed distraction for her.

"Has anyone heard from Mike, Mac, or Jimmy?" I asked.

Then suddenly everyone got quiet and shared the same worried face, so I knew something was wrong. Not this again. "Where is she?" I asked sternly. "Stop keeping secrets from me. I'm either part of this family or I'm not. If I am, then share the bad news already."

Kristy spilled right away. But she likes to gossip, so she couldn't wait to tell me. "They found Susan's body in her car," she announced. "She was shot and killed in the driver's seat. Sonja wasn't in the car. I'm so sorry. I know you two were close, are close I mean. I'm sure she's going to be okay."

My heart sank. This was not the news I was hoping for. Sonja could be anywhere. And Lola could be lurking outside, and no one would even know. The thought of that scared the crap out of me. I can't have her anywhere near our family, and especially near Willow.

Somehow the image in my mind is never how it really is. I pictured me and Mike together at the hospital when Willow was born. I pictured the family gathered around, celebrating her birth. And while everyone is happy that she has arrived, we're all grim because of Sonja being missing, and now worry as we wait to see what happens next with Lola. Always so much going on. Will it ever end?

I returned to my room so I could think in private. I just held Willow, wondering if I'm making another mistake. Wondering how I can be a good mother to her if I'm always on the run from a life that I can't seem to escape. Even from the grave, James seems to be everywhere. The people who work for him are not human. They can't be. A real person would experience remorse and see how wrong it is to torment a family.

Right?

I heard Mac and Mike come in. When I went to greet them, they were both solemn. Mac hugged me and his mama as if he had been defeated. My eyes filled with tears. I hate seeing him this way.

Mike hugged me and then took Willow from my arms. "She's so beautiful like her mama," he said as he kissed her. I smiled softly. *It feels so wrong to be excited about our daughter*, I thought, *when Sonja is still missing*.

"Any news on Sonja?" I asked.

"No," Mike, "said but they're sending a sheriff over to her place in Texas for a welfare check. I doubt they find anything." Mac just looked beat down. He appears to have aged ten years overnight. I can't imagine what he's going through, or Sonja for that matter. I feel so helpless.

Mac stood and told us he was going to shower and rest for a few hours. Then he's heading back out.

Nobody knows Lola better than me, I thought to myself. I need to think. Where would she go if she's planning an attack? She's ruthless and thinks I should pay for James's death and the demise of their life together. After pondering it for some time, I am certain the attack will most definitely be here, on our own land. There is no doubt in my mind. She would want me to suffer. She would want the family to suffer. It's not like we've been hiding. The truth is, we have become careless. Going into town more often and lightening the reins on our security. It happened slow, but it has surely happened. We need to find out who helped her escape from prison. Mac and Mike have been so worried about Sonja, that no one has investigated how Lola escaped from a maximum-security prison. Someone had to help her. Find that person, we'll get our first real lead.

A bit later, I decided to talk to Mike about what I was thinking. "I would bet my life that Lola is coming here," I told him. "I know her, none of you do. Her mission in life is to now take my life as punishment for killing James. She's angry. They clearly know where we are, or they could not have gotten to Sonja."

"I agree," Mike said. Mac also nodded in agreement, just as he walked back in the room announcing that he couldn't sleep. "I'll book a flight to Texas in the morning. It's a start. I think I'll pay a visit to Lola's father in prison while I'm there. Maybe he'll give her up if he knows she could get killed."

"It's a good thought, we'll see what happens. And brother?" Mac said to Mike. "I think you need to stay here with your wife. We need all the protection we can get on the home front. I'll take one of Jimmy's guys with me."

Mike instantly agreed. I'm sure he's worried about leaving Willow with Lola on the loose.

The entire family slept in the living room, following the safety in numbers rule. I held Willow most of the night. She only woke once, and Mama came to get her. I don't think Mama is getting much sleep, but she doesn't seem to mind, she likes to help and stay busy. It keeps her mind off of our current situation. Now the waiting and worrying will take over for all of us.

Mac was up at the crack of dawn. I heard a helicopter in the near distance. I got up to go see him in the kitchen. Everyone else was still sleeping. Kristy was holding Willow. I don't remember her coming to get her, but it was sweet to see her holding her. Baby Willow is going to have a life filled with love and family. The life I always wanted for myself, will never be a question for her. I took one last glance at them, smiled to myself, and then went to the kitchen to see Mac.

"Good morning, Mac. How are you holding up?" I asked.

"Good morning. About as well as can be expected," he replied. "I can't imagine what she's going through. She was mad at me before; now if she survives she'll hate me, and how can I blame her? I went back on my word. I promised to leave the DEA. And look what happened. How will I ever forgive myself?"

"Mac, we'll find her. And when we do, she'll forgive you. I know it. We're the fabulous four, we'll figure it out." He gave me a hug and a halfhearted smile.

"I thought you were catching a flight? How did you manage to get the helicopter on such short notice?" I asked.

"Jimmy pulled another favor. I'm in debt to him forever. He's a good man and a great friend."

"Yes, he is," I agreed. "I forgave him for the jab on the flight," I said with a warm smile.

"Well, I'm glad you two worked through it," Mac said.

Just then the chopper landed. Apparently Jimmy is going to drop Mac off and return. He said Jimmy will come back for him when Mac finds what he's looking for. Mike and Mama joined us just then. We all hugged, and then Mac got in the helicopter.

"I'll call you as soon as we land," he hollered to Mike. Mike gave him the thumbs up. And then in a less than a few minutes, they were gone. Anxiety overload is pretty much where I'm at.

I went back to the family room. Kristy was awake and so was Willow. Kristy was feeding her. I walked over to get her, but Kristy said she's got it handled. I thanked her and asked if she would mind if I took a quick shower.

"Oh, no, not at all. Take as long as you need," she said. "I'm bonding with my niece," she said with a smile. I kissed Kristy on the cheek and headed to the shower. I just love her; I love them all, actually. What would having a new baby be like if we didn't have all of this support? It would be so much harder, downright exhausting for sure.

Dune got up and followed me to the bathroom. "Poor little guy! Are you missing me? I'm so sorry you haven't had the attention you are used to." I picked him up and his licks said it all. Another lick to my teeth! Yuck! "I'm going to quit talking to you when I'm holding you if that behavior continues," I told him. Not that he understood a word I said. Anyway, I kissed him on the head and then put him down and turned on my shower water. I made it really hot and grabbed my lavender wash. *Oh, this feels so good.* I just stood there for the longest time. I hate this "off" feeling. I hope they find Lola and end this nightmare. It's like a rain cloud that keeps hovering over me, waiting to erupt in a scary storm.

CHAPTER SEVEN

After my shower, I tidied my room but then I felt weak. It's only been a few days since giving birth. I guess I'm not up for all of this just yet. Mike walked in as I was starting to sit. He must have been able to read my facial expressions. He came rushing to help me and asked if I was okay. "I'm fine," I replied. "Just did a little too much too soon I think. A few more days and I'll be back to normal." He got that look in his eyes, as if that meant we could make love already. "Slow down there, cowboy," I said, laughing. "I'm gonna need a little more time for all that."

"I'll settle for a kiss then," he said, flashing his incredible smile. I leaned into him and kissed him passionately.

I whispered, "I can't wait to make love to you."

"Me either," he whispered back.

"But…right now we need to go get our daughter. She probably doesn't know who her parents are," I said, laughing.

"True," he said in agreement. "I'll go get her and maybe we can all rest for a bit. I'm exhausted too," he added. Dune stood up on his back legs, as if to say *I'm in too!* Mike lifted him into bed and then left to get our baby girl. I could be deliriously happy if it weren't for this situation with Sonja.

"Please be okay," I prayed.

Surprisingly, we all slept a solid five hours. When we woke, I could smell something cooking, something yummy. I pulled my hair back and brushed my teeth. Mike peed, and then our little family headed towards the kitchen. Dune took off to join the other pups. All seven of them were together again and they are all so excited. They're oblivious to what's really going on all around them. Still too young, I think, to have any kind of real instincts.

Jimmy had his pup there as well as one of the guys on Jimmy's crew. Mike let them go out back to their fenced yard, to run off some of their energy. Between puppies, kids, and a baby, it was mayhem around here.

Mama was cooking ham, pancakes, and scrambled eggs. I'm starving. I offered to help but she wouldn't hear of it. Mama cooks when she's stressed or when something is not right. Not that we want her to be stressed, but I can say we all love to eat, so it's pretty happy here when Mama cooks. I have certainly gained a few pounds, and not just from having a baby. *I better get this under control,* I was thinking to myself but quickly decided I'll think about it tomorrow as Mama put the first batch of pancakes on the table. *I'll pass on pancakes,* said no one ever in this family. I smiled.

After our very late breakfast, I fed Willow and then rocked her for a bit. She just stared at me. I wonder what her little mind was thinking. I'm sure she knows I'm her mom, but what about all this chaos and all these people? Someone different is holding her all the time. Yet, she's so quiet and only cries if she's hungry or wet. I guess this will be normal for her. She'll get to grow up in beautiful chaos. She'll be one of the lucky ones who gets to experience the joys of a big, loving family.

I put Willow in her crib once she fell asleep and turned her monitor on. Then I headed to the living room. It was quiet. No one was there. I wanted to go look for them but I wasn't comfortable leaving Willow, so I decided to go back to our room. I saw the door to my room close out of the corner of my eye. *Hmmm…* I thought. I assumed it was Mike, so I opened the door. It was Sonja. I was in disbelief, total shock. I only stared at her for a moment. "Oh my god, you're okay," I said to her. "What happened? Where have you been?"

She started to cry. "I don't even know how to tell you. I've dishonored this family. I'm ashamed and embarrassed."

"Sonja, what can be so bad that you can't tell me? And why didn't you tell me you were leaving? I thought we were friends. Best friends, actually. Everyone has been so worried about you," almost as if I was scolding her.

She took a few deep breaths and then started explaining. "The day I left I called the beauty shop to see if Susan was working. She and I have been friends for a long time, so I wanted to talk to her about Mac. She knows our on-again, off-again history, so I just missed talking to her. I was really pissed at Mac over going back with the DEA. She and I had a bet. When I told her Mac and I were getting married, she said the marriage wouldn't last a year; she was right. So I called to tell her she was right and about how angry I was with Mac.

"You and Mike were so excited about the baby, and rightfully so, so it just didn't feel right to unload our troubles on you."

"You still should have told me."

"I know, I'm so sorry," she said. "Anyway, the shop apparently had been bugged. And I know I'm not supposed to be talking to people from our past right now, but that's easier said than done. Anyway, they were able to listen to the calls made to and from the shop, and in turn track Susan, which led right back to me and the cabin. It was her idea to come and get me. When she arrived to pick me up, they followed us. Susan noticed them in the rear-view mirror almost immediately after she picked me up, so we sped up and then they did to. Then…the chase was on. They started ramming her car and firing shots at the tires. We were so scared. The last hit ran us right off the road." She paused and took a deep breath, still crying.

"I don't get how that disrespects the family," I said. "That doesn't sound like anything to be ashamed of. It's not like you could control what was happening."

"Oh, it is, trust me," Sonja continued. "We hit a tree after the impact of the last hit. The airbags deployed, and somehow Susan was stuck in her seat. Anyway, when I realized I couldn't get her out, I just left her there."

Tears were pouring as she was trying to tell me what had happened.

Sonja continued talking. "I took off running and hid in a hollowed-out tree. I was only thinking of myself. They looked for me for about a half hour but couldn't find me. The man who appeared to be in charge hollered if I didn't come out on the count of three, he would put a bullet in her head.

I was terrified, so I just stayed hidden. On three, he shot her in the head just as he said he would. I'll never forget the fear that was in her eyes. How could I do that to her? She came here to get me because I had a tantrum over Mac. She's a single mom of two boys, and now she's dead. Her kids are orphans. I didn't know what to do next, so I stayed in there all night in case they were still close by. At sunrise this morning, I started making my way back to the cabin. I was trying to crouch in the fields so that if they came back, they wouldn't be able to spot me. Oh god, what have I done?"

"It could have happened to anyone," I told her. "No one plans to get stuck in their seatbelt during an accident. It must have malfunctioned. And if you would have come out, you would most likely be dead too."

"I need to go get her kids," Sonja cried. "How am I going to face Mac?"

"Trust me," I said, "Mac will be very happy to see you. He's been a mess. I've never seen him this way."

Just then, Willow started to cry. I went and picked her up.

Sonja put both hands over her mouth as she gasped in shock. She had no idea that Willow had arrived. "She's early. Is everything okay with her?"

"She's healthy and perfect," I proudly announced. "You can hold her."

Sonja picked her up and held her briefly, and then handed her back to me. She congratulated me while crying once more. "I have disappointed every person I love, including you. I'm so sorry I wasn't here when she was born. I'm sorry for all the stress I know I have caused for everyone. I just can't face any of them right now."

"Yes, you can," I said, "and you will. I'm calling Mike now." I picked up my phone, called him, and told him I needed him asap.

I looked at Sonja; she was so disheveled and dirty. Her last few days have been hell just like they have been for the rest of us. I hugged her and told her, "It's going to be okay."

When Mike arrived, I filled him in on what happened with Sonja. He then called Mac to tell him, "We have Sonja and she's okay."

She and Mac spoke for just a few minutes. She told him, "I'll tell you everything when you get here, but right now, I need you to go and get Susan's two children. Please let us know when you have them," she stated in a panicked voice. Mac agreed to go pick them up and give us a call once that happened. "They're eleven and thirteen. Susan left them alone when she drove here from Texas. She said they're old enough to be alone for a few days. I didn't question her about her kids, I was only thinking of myself and how mad I was. What did I do?" is all she kept saying over and over. She was now inconsolable and irrational.

"Mike, I think we need to call Jimmy for one of those shots," I said. "She's not okay."

"Are you sure?" he asked. "You weren't happy when Jimmy gave one to you," he replied.

"True, but no one asked me, they just did it," I said. "That matters."

I went and grabbed some of Sonja's night clothes and told her to take a quick shower. Somehow, she did manage to shower and get dressed, but she's a mess. I told her we were giving her something to help her sleep for a while. I promised to be there when she woke up. She agreed, and

Jimmy did his thing. She was out. He carried her to her and Mac's room.

I finally feel better knowing she's okay. Worrying about Lola coming for us seems so small in comparison to the worry and fear we had for Sonja's safety. Our family is now once again complete. We're all safe, for the time being anyway.

Chapter Eight

It's the middle of the night and I'm wide awake. There seems to be a pattern of me being awake in the wee hours of the night. Sleep is not coming so easy for me lately. My mind just won't shut down. Willow is sleeping great for a newborn so I should be sleeping easy too. I can't stop thinking about Lola. How can there ever be peace for any of us with her out there somewhere. I just don't know what she's up to, what she's planning. No one else seems as concerned as I am. It makes me wonder if they know more than they are sharing. Mac and Mike are still in protective mode when it comes to me. I wish they could see how much stronger I am now.

Mike sat up. "Why aren't you sleeping?" he asked.

"You know how I am when things are off, I don't sleep."

"Yes, I do," he said. "What can I do to ease your worries?"

"Has anyone checked on Sonja lately?" I asked him.

"Not since the last time you sent me, which was about an hour and a half ago," Mike stated as he looked at his watch.

"She's fine," he added. "There's a guard at her door. There are men all over. We've got this," Mike assured. "You need to get some sleep." Just then Willow started crying. "I'll get her."

"No," I replied. "I'm wide awake, I'll get her. You can sleep. There's no need for both of us to be up all night." Mike lay back down and was back to sleep in no time. I can always tell when he's asleep because his snore is more like a roar. I smiled as I was thinking that. It's funny how sometimes I find his snore to be comforting and other times I want to bonk him in the head. Why is that? I almost laughed out loud as I was leaning towards a bonk in the head. Instead of a head bonking, I opted to watch him sleep. Willow didn't seem to be bothered by his snore at all. She went right back to sleep after her bottle. I am noticing a trend, though. She's not as happy if she's not being held. I'm glad that so many of us share in this responsibility.

I put Willow back in her crib and decided I was going to make breakfast. I made homemade biscuits, sausage, sausage gravy, fried potatoes, and a fresh fruit platter. By the time I was done with everything, it was almost eight A.M. and everyone was starting to make their way to the kitchen. Mama was especially happy to see that she didn't have to cook. She poured herself a cup of coffee as she kissed me on the cheek. She said, "You cooked, we'll give Kristy and the girls clean-up duty," and then she gave me a wink. She laughed at herself like she just came up with some brilliant plan. I see where Mike gets it. His humor comes from her. It made me laugh too.

Anyway, I sat back and watched the chaos begin just like normal, plates, being passed, and lots of conversation. But everyone suddenly stopped.

I realized we're still missing Mac and Sonja. Mama must've seen my face turn to sadness because she came over to me and said, "Go check on her. I'll make sure everybody has what they need." I thanked Mama and gave her a quick hug and then I headed straight to Sonja's room.

I opened the door to peek in, and she was laying there awake. Her eyes were filled with tears. "Hey," I said, "I'm glad to see you're awake. Breakfast is ready. We'd love for you to join us."

"I don't know if I can," she said.

"Sonja, we have to talk about this. You didn't do anything wrong. We are all so thankful that you are okay. I am so sorry for what happened to Susan. I'm sure she must've been someone special for you to call her first when you were upset with Mac."

"She was a good friend to me. We worked at the shop together for a long time, so we know a lot about each other. I should've never called her and put her life in danger," she said, tearing up. "I just didn't think about it. And now her kids will have no parents. Their father has never been in the picture. Susan never talked about him, and I don't know who he is or where he might be."

"Mac told you he would get them, and you know he will. We'll probably be hearing from him any time. But for now, your family is waiting for you to have breakfast. Please come and join us."

She agreed and got out of bed. "I'm gonna brush my teeth and change my clothes and I'll be right there."

"I'll wait, if that's okay with you."

She smiled softly and went to the bathroom and closed the door. A few minutes passed and she came out of the bathroom. She freshened up and looked much better.

I put my arm around her, and we walked to the kitchen where everyone had fixed their plates, but no one had started eating. My heart melted. Sonja teared up as she thanked everyone for waiting. I could see the pride on Mama's face. Just as we were having that special moment, Kristy blurted it out, "Hungry here." Everyone laughed, and the chaos resumed. Mama was proud of me today. I knew it. I felt it. I was proud of myself today. Being able to comfort Sonja, take care of my baby with little to no sleep, and pull off a meal like this is pretty awesome.

Just then Mike's phone rang, and he got "the look" from his mama. She doesn't allow phones at the table, but this was one call Mike needed to take. It was Mac. Everyone became silent. "Uh-huh, okay, sounds good," was all we could get from Mike's side of the conversation. After he hung up with Mac, Mike announced, "They have the kids and they're on their way back." Everyone cheered for what we could consider a victory. I was so happy, but no one was happier than Sonja. I hugged her. She did actually eat a little bit too, so that's a good thing.

After breakfast, Mama told Kristy she had clean up duty. "What?" Kristy replied.

"You heard me. The girls can help you," Mama added. And just like that, the three of them started cleaning up. Everyone thanked me for breakfast and went on about their business. Pops was holding Willow.

I was exhausted, I realized. I declared a nap was in order for myself. Mike said, "No worries, I've got her." I looked at him and remembered he doesn't do poop diapers. "What?" he said?

His mama smiled and said, "We've got her," so she knew exactly what I was worried about. What would he do without his mama? I had this image of him gagging, choking, and possibly passing out because he had a poop diaper. I kissed him and headed to the bathroom for a quick shower and then some much-needed rest.

I did actually sleep this time. The relief of knowing Sonja was okay, and now the boys, is absolutely wonderful. Best news of the day! Lola being on the loose is the only thing that can make me lose sleep. We have to get her. The sooner the better.

Chapter Nine

I awoke several hours later to the sound of a nearby helicopter. It's so loud. I was still so tired and struggling to stay awake when I realized that it was Mac with the kids. They must be landing. Do the kids even know about their mom yet? Who is going to tell them, and will they be okay?

Panic! I jumped up. That old familiar feeling keeps coming back. And with it, a racing heart that feels like it's going to burst out of my chest. I do worry that someday it's going to be real.

I ran outside. Mac and Sonya were hugging. They were so happy to see each other, and it was such a beautiful sight to see. Mac kept telling her how sorry he was, and she was doing the same. In hindsight, I think they both were a bit hasty in how they handled the news about Lola's escape. Which led me back to my own reaction. I too, was a bit hasty I realized, and certainly unfair to Mike. I feel really bad now, and I'm going to offer him an honest and deep apology at the first opportunity. He deserves that.

I walked over to Mac and hugged him. I was happy to see him too. The two boys were just standing there. They had no idea what was going on. I was getting ready to head over to them, but Mama beat me to it. *No one better*, I thought to myself. Mama put her hands on their shoulders and started walking with them. I knew she would have some profound words of wisdom to comfort them when they find out about their mom.

My thoughts wandered off a bit as I watched her walk away with them. I wondered if they would blame Sonya for their mother's death even though she didn't have anything to do with it. Would they see it for the accident that it was? And, legally, what will happen to them? No one knows who the father is, so maybe our family can adopt them? So much to think about, but I guess for now we just need to make them feel safe, comfortable, and a part of our family.

From a distance, it seemed that Mac and Sonya have reconciled. I'm sure she'll fill me in later. Right now, I need to go find Mike. I need to make things right with him too.

"There you are," I said. "Been looking for you." He was holding Willow, and she was asleep in his arms. "What a beautiful sight you are to me," I said to him.

I leaned over to kiss him and then I asked him to put Willow in her crib. "I'm not sure she's going to like that; she's been a bit fussy when I've tried to put her down. I think she's spoiled already," he said, laughing.

"I'm sure she is," I agreed, "but she'll be fine." I watched him kiss our baby and then lay her down. *He's a great father already*, I thought to myself.

After he put her down, he turned to look at me. I was looking at him too with deep admiration. I started to speak. "Mike, I wanted to tell you I'm so sorry for how I behaved when finding out about Lola's escape. It's not like you had anything to do with it. I was just so afraid of losing you if you went back to the FBI. But the truth is, it's wrong of me to think that I should be able to decide that for you. I love you with everything in me regardless of your choice to stay or leave the FBI. You and Willow are my everything, essentially my whole world. I want you to do what makes you happy, and if being in the FBI is it for you, then I understand and will support whatever you decide."

He kissed me with a deep and meaningful kiss. I want him so bad right now and I know he feels it too.

He pulled away from me. "We have to stop before there's no turning back.

"Jenna," he continued, "you don't have to worry. I'm not going back to the FBI, but I appreciate what you said. However, you don't have to be sorry. In hindsight, I should've told you as soon as we found out about Lola, but my first instinct was to protect you. That will always be my first reaction. So I'm sorry, but I can't promise that I'll never do it again, but I can promise to love you forever. I can promise to protect you and Willow no matter what."

"What's this about, Jenna?" Mike asked. "Why are you apologizing now? It's been a few days."

"I know, but seeing Mac and Sonja reunite today made me realize how ridiculous I was being. There is nothing more important than us and this family. The entire family."

"God, how did I ever find you?" Mike asked.

We held each other for a few minutes before getting up to go find Mac and Sonja.

We went to the kitchen, where we found Mac and Sonya sitting with Pops, having coffee. "Have a seat," Mac said. We both sat. I could see Mama walking towards the cabin with both boys. They had been crying no doubt. Their eyes were puffy and red. My heart instantly felt broken for them. Sonja started crying when she saw them. She and I held hands until Mama opened the door and the three of them walked in.

Mama spoke first. "This here is Brandon, and this is Aidan. They know what happened to their mom, and they'll be staying with us for a while." Both boys were just standing there staring at all of us. I can't imagine what they are feeling right now.

I stood and introduced myself. "Hi, I'm Jenna," I said. "I am so sorry about your mom. But we are all here if you need anything, please don't hesitate to ask."

Both boys were sniffing and said thank you.

Then Sonja stood and went to hug them. "I'm so sorry," she said, her eyes once again filling with tears. "Your mom loved you so much. We can't replace your beautiful mama, but Mac and I are going to take good care of you, I promise."

It was an emotional afternoon for everyone. Mama, being the cheerleader that she is, asked, "How about pizza? Everyone getting hungry?" Lots of yeses being thrown out. While the boys are emotional and upset, Mama was the perfect person to tell them. I can see the trust they already have in her. That's the best news we can hope for right now.

Mac and Sonja took the boys to their room for tonight. They're sleeping in the living room. Right now, there are only five bedrooms. Mac and Mike are going to clean the attic out tomorrow and make a space for them. Being young teenagers, they can't stay in Mac and Sonja's room.

A bit later, I could smell the aroma of Mama's lemon cake, mixed with a fresh Italian pizza. "Oh goodness, it smells good in here," I told Mama upon entering the kitchen.

"Thanks, dear. I'm hoping to give these boys a nice warm welcome."

"You're a good woman," I told her.

"Despite losing their mom, they'll find a family here, one full of love and happiness," Mama said. "It's the best possible outcome, given what's happened."

"I agree, Mama, but what about the legalities of keeping them here?"

"We'll figure all that out in due time. It has to be declared that there are no living relatives to take them. I already have a call in to our attorney so hopefully I will hear back from him soon. Sonya is pretty sure there is no extended family.

"Fingers crossed," I said. "How long on dinner? I'm starving."

"Not much longer. Grab some plates and napkins. I'm going to pull the first two pies out in a minute. The next two are going in. Can you summon everyone to dinner, please?"

I did as Mama asked, but with this many people it's like trying to corral a herd of cows. Note to self: buy Mama a dinner bell.

Kristy arrived first, holding Willow. She handed her to me. I kissed her tiny cheek. *I love this baby girl so much*, I was thinking to myself.

The crowd came rushing at the call of dinner, including the guards. It was so loud but Willow doesn't seem to mind. I'm just glad she's adjusting well to all of this chaos.

Chapter Ten

Dinner went well, and our two newest family members seemed to fit right in. I'm convinced that anyone can fit in with this family. Aiden and Brandon were quietly watching everyone. It seemed as though they were taking it all in. I'm certain by the look on their faces they've lived a pretty quiet life. Sonja handed each of them a slice of pizza and a Coke. It didn't take long for them to finish it and ask for another. About halfway through dinner they were joining the conversation. *This is great progress*, I thought. I gave Sonja a look, to let her know she's doing great. She gave me a sad smile in return. Somehow, she needs to see that the tragedy of what happened is a gift in disguise. Mac never settled down long enough to have children, and Sonja couldn't have them. While it's tragic they lost their mother, a good, loving family can assume that role. Hopefully, with time, they can see the miracle of it all and move past the sadness they are feeling.

Pleased with my own assessment of this situation, I don't want to diminish what happened to their mother. We'll let time do its thing, the chips fall where they may so to speak. And just maybe, Sonja can be relieved of the guilt she feels.

After dinner, Sonja and I did the dishes. She opened up about feeling responsible for Susan's boys. "I would give anything for a do-over," she said.

"You know Sonja, I used to wish for do overs all the time. Unfortunately, as with most things in life, there's not an option for do-overs. Once a decision is made, it's generally one we have to live with. But we need to see the good in every situation. There's no answer to why this happened. But now there is reason to overcome."

"I think you are exactly who I needed in my life Jenna. Thank you for the kind words. They mean more to me than you can imagine. I need to stop feeling sorry for myself and put on my big girl pants. We have two boys to finish raising," Sonja declared.

We hugged for the longest time.

"So how is Mac feeling about all of this? You know, about becoming a dad?" I asked.

"Actually, pretty good," Sonja said. "And, honestly, better than I expected. Since I'm not able to have children, it was never a topic of discussion. He's been married to his job, so he didn't think kids were in the life plan for him. That always worked for us. But now, we have these boys. I only hope the court grants us custody. This whole thing with Lola could hinder it for us." I looked at her as my eyes began filling with tears. Once again, my past could cause a problem for them.

"Once again, me being here could endanger another family. How can I be okay with this?"

"No, no," she said. "I wasn't blaming you. None of this is on you. Mac and Mike chose their line of work. This is what they do. They save people, and thank God they saved you. I love you."

"I love you too," I replied, still sobbing. "I know you're right. My mind automatically always goes there and then to my son. It's just hard to not wish that some things had turned out differently. Realizing do-overs aren't an option, I can only wish, right?"

"Trust me," she said. "I'm in that boat too. Now and forever, I'm certain. I guess we both have heavy baggage to carry. Let's just promise each other, when the load is too much, we'll be there for each other, no matter what."

"I promise," I told her. We hugged once again and then decided to join the rest of the family.

As soon as we got to the family room, Mama said, "I was just coming to look for you girls. We're going to have movie night. I think our entire family could use a distraction."

"I agree," I told Mama. "I think it sounds fun and relaxing." I looked over to Mike. He was holding Willow in our big, round double chair. Well, it's not really our chair, but we sort of claimed it. No one else sits there except us. I went to sit beside him and kissed Willow on the head. Mike put his free arm around me. We snuggled in for what I'm pretty sure will be family sleepover night. *So nice*, I thought, even if Lola still hovers in my mind.

At some point during the movie, I drifted off to sleep. I woke up a few hours later and looked around. Everyone was asleep, and somehow, Kristy was holding Willow again. Maybe Willow woke up and neither Mike nor I heard her?

I'll have to ask her when she wakes up. I got up to go to the bathroom and I saw Jimmy on the phone. *Who could he possibly be talking to at this hour?* I thought.

I peed and then went to the kitchen to ask him. I'm thinking something must be going on.

"Hey," I said to him.

"Hey," he said back. "It's a bit early for you to be up, isn't it?" he commented.

"It is, but I could say the same for you," I replied.

"Normally that would be true, but tonight it's my turn on the night watch, so I'll sleep at sunrise."

"Ahh," I said. "But who were you just talking to?"

"Me," Mac said as he joined us in the kitchen.

"Okay," I said, "so something is going on."

"Not exactly but kind of," Mac said.

"So it's going to be that kind of chat," I said sarcastically.

He laughed at me. It felt like old times for a minute. Sometimes I think he just spouts off something to get my panties in a bunch, so I just gave him the eye roll. Then we all laughed.

"Seriously, what is going on, guys?" I asked a second time.

"I'm heading out," Mac said. "I'm going to see Lola's dad. I was going to see him last trip, but we had an emergency diversion with the kids. Lola has been way too quiet, and that makes me nervous. I'm hoping when I tell him that she'll most likely be killed in a forced apprehension, he'll make the right choice and tell us where she is."

"Don't count on it," I said. "They think they're invincible. And why wouldn't they? Look what they've gotten away with for all these years. I've accepted that she'll just be a thorn in my life."

"I don't like thorns," Mac replied. "Therefore, a thorn in my life isn't an option. This has to be the next step in finding her. I can be relentless too."

"Well, I like your attitude," I told him.

"Thanks," he said.

In the distance, I heard the helicopter. Mac grabbed his black bag and headed outside. I ran out after him because I feel like I need to say something.

"Mac, please be safe and don't stay gone too long. Our family isn't the same without you." He leaned down to hug me.

"Does Sonja know you're leaving?" I asked?

"She does," he replied. "She told me to go get them! Jenna, can you give this to Mike for me?" Mac asked. "He knows what it is." I took the paper and folded it in my hand. Then he turned and left. I looked at the paper before going in. It's an address, but who's address is it and where is it?

My thoughts went back to him leaving. This man is a hero. He continues to risk his life for all of us. How many times will he have to save us before it's over? Or will it ever be over?

I went back inside the cabin after the helicopter left. Mama was sitting at the table. "Good morning," I said to her.

"Good morning," she replied. "I see Mac left without giving me a proper goodbye," she added.

"I think the plan was to sneak off without telling anyone except Sonja," I told her. "But, unfortunately for him, I couldn't sleep. I'm pretty sure he's on a mission to end it this time by convincing Lola's father to disclose her location. I personally can't see that happening, but it would be great if it did."

"Yes it would," she agreed. "I'm getting old, I feel it more and more every day. We'll never have peace if this isn't resolved." I gave Mama a hug and then left.

I hate what I've done to this family. I need to find her myself and resolve the problem I created. She's close by. I can feel it.

Feeling determined, in that moment, I knew what I had to do. In order for this to be over for all of us, I will have to be the one to make it happen. Even if that means I could possibly not survive. At least Willow and the family would be safe. And that in itself is worth the risk. It's been decided. I'll find her, I have no choice.

CHAPTER ELEVEN

Mike and Willow are still asleep. I threw a few things in my backpack and took some money from the safe. I grabbed two guns, a knife, and the paper that Mac gave me for Mike and threw them in my bag. I also took a small first aid kit and a bear spray. Just in case. Lastly, I grabbed a few water bottles, a box of granola bars, and a few changes of clothes. Hopefully, I have a decent head start before anyone else wakes up.

Still dark outside, I started walking as fast as I could. The wheat grass is tall and wet. I'm so glad I put on my cargo pants and a sweatshirt, although my pants seem a bit tighter than I remember. Note to self: eat less pancakes. I did bring my burner phone, just in case, but it's turned off.

I've now been walking for about an hour and a half. I'm starting to feel the pain of having Willow. I'm guessing my body isn't quite ready for what I'm doing but it's now or never. I'm going to mow through. I have to.

I heard a truck in the near distance. I have to be getting close to the road. I crossed the bridge over the river and stopped to admire its beauty. It really is breathtaking here. I could see a mama deer and her baby getting a drink of water. The fog was starting to lift, and a glimpse of sunshine is starting to rise and peek through the trees.

I took a moment to get a drink of water for myself and then took my sweatshirt off. It is starting to warm up nicely. I love the feel of the warm sun on my skin. For a brief second, I thought about the beach. The smell and the warmth, I absolutely love it. When this is over, a beach trip will be necessary for my mental health. It seems my mental state is rapidly deteriorating.

Getting back to reality, I started walking again. *Faster*, I told myself. Not too long later, I could see the road. I made it.

Now what? Well, I guess I didn't think this through, I thought. I took a gun out of my backpack and made sure it was loaded. I put it in the right pocket of my cargo pants. I'm going to hitchhike. Yep, I have officially lost my mind. I don't even know where I'm going yet. If Jimmy were here, he'd definitely be giving me a shot and then dropping me at the closest mental health facility. And I would deserve it. I know this is crazy, and a very bad idea, but it has to be done.

I continued walking once I was on the road, but not for long. A semi-truck was headed this way. I felt silly as I put my thumb up in the air. The driver started slowing down and then pulled over. I walked to the passenger side of his truck and opened the door. An older guy was sitting in the seat with a tiny Chihuahua. It started barking at me. The driver asked me where I was headed. I told him I wasn't sure yet, but I needed a lift. He told me to hop in. I climbed up in the truck and was suddenly terrified. What the hell was I thinking? This guy could be a deranged killer. These are the kind of situations that land a special episode of the missing but stupid. I've watched these shows, one after another, show after show of missing and murdered. Will I be the next missing persons case? Will I get my own special episode?

He must have sensed that I was afraid. He introduced himself as Elmer, and his dog as Ella. She just kept staring at me like she was protecting her master. *How cute*, I thought.

"So, what's a pretty lady like you doing out on a road like this all alone? It's dangerous for you to be hitchhiking and taking rides with old men like me," he added.

He seemed nice enough, and he's old. I'm pretty sure I can take him if he's not on the up and up.

I agreed with him that I shouldn't be hitchhiking, "but I'm doing this to protect my family," I told him.

He looked at me, confused. So I continued.

I don't know why, but I ended up sharing my whole life story with him, leaving out the part about Willow. He doesn't need to know about her yet.

When I finished telling him everything, he simply stated, "This would make a great movie! Too bad I'm not a producer." We both laughed as I agreed with him.

"Do you make it a habit of picking up hitchhikers?" I asked him.

"Actually, no, you're my first," he replied. "I only stopped because I was worried about your safety. Weird, right? You could have been a serial killer," he said, laughing.

I didn't think about things from his perspective. He could be just as scared of me as I was of him. I reassured him I wasn't a killer and really just needed a ride.

It's been almost two hours since I got in the truck with him, and we've been chatting the entire time. Elmer asked me if I was hungry. "There's a diner up the road that I like to frequent. My girlfriend Patty works there."

He seemed a little old to have a girlfriend, but I told him food sounded great! And besides, I need to pee.

I saw the diner up ahead. So far, he seems like a nice man. Surely, if he's taking me to a diner where his girlfriend works, he's an honest man. I've got my gun just in case. And lucky for me, I shoot pretty good now thanks to Mike and Mac. The entire family shoots often down by the river. We're all ready in case trouble finds us.

He pulled into the diner parking lot. Several other trucks were already parked there. We got out and went inside. He seemed to know a lot of people in there. Lots of *hi's* and *good to see ya's* going on. All eyes were on me for sure. Probably wondering what I was doing with him. What if they thought I was a prostitute? Surely not. I am not dressed anything like a hooker would typically dress. *No way I could be mistaken as a working girl*, I thought to myself.

Elmer walked over to the counter and had a seat. I sat beside him. A woman came over and gave him a quick kiss and then she looked at me. "This is my girl, Patty," he said as he introduced us. She looked to be in her sixties maybe but still very attractive. He appeared to be older than her, but they seemed to really like each other. I felt safer already. He explained to her that I was in a bit of a pickle and needed a lift. She seemed okay with it after we chatted for a few minutes.

Elmer and I both ordered biscuits and gravy, with fried potatoes and coffee to drink. I noticed the dinner bell on the counter. In fact, there were a couple of them. I asked Elmer what they were for. He said, "She makes them and sells them on the side with her diner logo." They're so cute. I want to make sure to purchase one for Mama before we leave.

"So have you figured out where you're heading?" he asked.

"Actually, yes," I said. "I've settled on Texas," I stated matter-of-factly. "The source of all of my problems is there. It's time to make things right."

"Well, I admire your courage," he said. "I can't take you all the way there, but I can get you most of the way." I thanked him and bought his breakfast, along with a dinner bell. I can't wait to give it to Mama. I wrapped it and securely placed it in my bag.

When we finished, he chatted with Patty for a few more minutes and then kissed her goodbye. He told her he'd see her in a few days.

We used the bathroom again and then got back in his truck and headed out.

I felt much more relaxed knowing he wasn't a serial killer. He was sweet. I liked him and Patty. My mind went back to the cabin. By now, they're probably all looking for me, wondering what happened. And I am positive none of them can understand what I'm thinking. Maybe when it's over they will get it.

My family is my world. I've been a prisoner for far too much of my life. I want to be free, and I mean really free.

Free to live, free to watch my baby grow up without having to look over my shoulder. But mostly, I want the entire family to be free from the burden that comes with me being there. I don't want them to carry the weight of keeping me safe any longer. I see the stress we're all under.

I heard Elmer say, "A penny for your thoughts?"

"Oh, I'm sorry," I said as I turned to look at him. "I'm not being very good company. I was just thinking about my family."

"I'm sure they're worried about you. It's not too late to change your mind," he said.

"I can't," I told him. I have to do this. Changing the subject, "Tell me about you and Patty. You've got yourself a real beauty," I said with a smile.

"My wife died about eight years ago," he said. "She had cancer, and she fought a long and hard battle before she passed away. We were married for forty-one years, and I just didn't know how to live without her. I went back to driving a truck about a year after she passed. I was tired of feeling sorry for myself and tired of being alone. One day, I pulled into the diner for the first time. Patty had found a tiny stray dog that had been hanging around the diner for a few days. She was feeding her but works too many hours to keep her permanently as a pet. She was asking patrons of the diner if someone could take her in. I agreed to take her but only if she agreed to go on a date with me." He was smiling as he was telling me about that day as if it were still fresh in his memory.

"Awe, that is such a sweet story," I told him, "but I am very sorry about your wife."

"That's okay," he said. "It was tough times then, but I made it through." He continued with his story. "After my third date with Patty, she told me she owned the diner and works lots of hours. It's been in business for twenty-nine years. Now I drive the same route so I can stop and see her often. The bonus is, they have the best coconut cream pie I've ever had," he said with a beaming smile. "She makes it fresh daily, her own recipe. Now, I spend my days off at her house or helping in the diner. It's a good life."

"Why haven't you married her?" I asked him.

"I think about it, but sometimes I still feel like I'm betraying my wife."

"Til death do us part means you're free to love again, and it's okay if you do," I told him. "I didn't know your wife, but I'm sure she wouldn't want you to be lonely."

"You're probably right," he said.

"I'm realizing that everyone has a curveball thrown at them in this game of life," I told him. "And maybe that's just life for all of us. We're presented with these obstacles to overcome, so you have to figure them out, all the while keeping up with the pace of everyday life. Otherwise, what would life be like without complications and hurdles to jump along with the happy perfect part of life? At the end of the day, I think it's all part of a balancing system."

"You could be on to something," he said.

I think we both felt some sort of admiration for each other. He's another piece of the puzzle to my life. I'm not sure what part he will play in my life in the future, but he's a significant part for right now. It's funny how that happens. I have a feeling that I'll be seeing him and Patty again when this is all over.

Chapter Twelve

I am getting tired and finally feel comfortable saying that I'm safe. "I'm going to close my eyes for a few minutes," I told Elmer. It wasn't long before I drifted off to sleep. Sometimes, when I'm being bounced around in Mike's truck, it just makes me so sleepy. I wonder if this is how a baby feels when they're being rocked?

I don't know how he's not tired, I thought when I woke up and saw that Elmer was still driving. He hasn't even mentioned being tired or needing a break. "Where are we?" I asked?

"Texas," he said.

I sat up straight, as if to be more focused. "I'm confused, I thought you couldn't take me the whole way?"

"Well," he said, "it just didn't feel right to drop you somewhere. There are too many crazy, weird people out there," he said, almost as if he were scolding me.

Another man that feels the need to protect me, I thought. I find that odd. I wonder if I play the role of a victim somehow when I talk to people. If I do, I need to change that. I am not a victim. I'm a Survivor. And I certainly do not want to be pitied or viewed as a victim.

"I'm so glad you're not one of the crazy ones, and thank you for being one of the good guys!" I reached over and squeezed his hand. Then I gave him the address to the mansion. All he knows is that it's a really big house. "Listen," I said to him, "I'm being serious. People that are with me or a part of my life tend to be in danger. I can't ask you to go there with me."

"You didn't ask," he said. "I volunteered, so I'll decide if a little bit of danger is going to scare me off. And I thought about it. I'm good to go."

I laughed at him. "Feisty," I said! I bet he was a lot of fun when he was young. "I'm glad I met you," I told him.

"Likewise," he said. "I'm always up for a new adventure."

"Well, you may just get more than you bargained for," I told him.

We continued chatting the rest of the way about a lot of things, insignificant things. It helped to make the time pass a little faster. It was dark when we finally arrived at the mansion. "Holy shit," he said when we turned into the driveway. "You were serious when you said it was a really big house. Damn, that's big," he added.

"I told you it was big. I just didn't tell you how big but I can assure you it's nothing special. I told you the truth about everything…almost," I continued.

"Almost?" he asked.

"I have a daughter," I told him. "Only a few weeks old. I'm doing this so she can be safe. So we can all be safe. I didn't tell you when I was telling you about myself, just in case you were a serial killer." We both laughed at the thought of him being any kind of killer.

"Having a child to protect is a game-changer," he said. "Let's do this." As we got closer to the front of the mansion, we could see the crime tape everywhere on the outside of the home and a sign that read. "No Trespassing—Government Property."

I used my key and went in anyway. "What are you hoping to find here?" he asked me.

"I need to find James's payroll information. I need proof of the attempt on my life, proof that Lola is deep in the drug world with her father. It would be somewhere that no one else would think to look. I am certain the FBI would have searched this place for the same information. But James was really smart. He always thought everything through. He was cold and calculating."

We went past the large foyer, and my heart sank. I stopped right where I was standing and let out a wail. The dried blood from my son was all over the wall where they shot him seventeen times. I started crying hysterically. My baby's dead. Elmer came to comfort me. Actually, he was holding me up as my knees began to buckle underneath me. I knew he died here, but actually seeing the place where he died and his blood on the wall brings the realization that's he's gone forever. There will be no do-overs, no second chances with my baby.

"Let's leave." Elmer said. "This place gives me the creeps and I don't like seeing you this upset."

"No, it's okay," I told him, pulling myself together. "It is a creepy place, so you're right to feel that way. Let's go upstairs and look around." Elmer agreed, but reluctantly.

Once upstairs, we went to James's office, and just as I had suspected, everything was gone. His file cabinets, his computers, and even his desk were gone.

The only room that appeared to be untouched was my room. The room where I was held prisoner for much of my adult life. I walked into the room and looked around. *I'm no longer any part of the broken girl who once lived in this space*, I thought to myself.

And then it hit me. It only made sense that James would hide something in here. A room where he knew it would be safe. I bet he watched me in here. While I was hiding things in the wall, so was he. I don't know why, but I just know it to be true.

"Start looking everywhere," I told Elmer. "Look for loose boards in the floors, walls, furniture, look under the bed and anywhere something could be hidden. Those files are here somewhere."

We started pulling up boards, emptying drawers, and turning furniture. I was almost frantic. We looked for nearly thirty minutes and then…there they were.

The files I've been looking for. The files I knew had to exist. "I need to make sure we find everything," I told Elmer. All this time, hiding right in front of me. The payroll files were rolled and stashed in the wrought iron bed frame. "Help me," I hollered to Elmer.

We started pulling the frame apart piece by piece. More documents were falling out. In the post, was a bag of money. A lot of money. I looked at Elmer and handed him the bag of money. "Take it," I told him. "You deserve it after all of this."

He smiled and said, "We'll discuss my cut later."

I smiled back at him and said, "Okay." The last section of the bedframe was taken apart. I put the papers in my backpack, deciding we could read them later. Elmer grabbed the money bag and we headed for the door.

I stopped just as I did before to take a look around the room. Hopefully the last look I'll ever have to take of this room or any room in this house. "What a sad and lonely place," I told Elmer.

"Creepy too," he added. "Let's get out of here."

We left in a hurry, and this time I held on to Elmer and closed my eyes as we passed the blood-stained wall. Once outside, we both ran to his truck, as if we couldn't get out of there fast enough. We were a few miles down the road before I could relax. I kept looking back to make sure we weren't being followed.

"I think we're all right," Elmer said, "other than my heart is racing like never before. These are probably not good activities for a guy my age. My ticker only has so many ticks left."

I laughed and said, "We'll try to find something more age appropriate on our next adventure. Let's get you home." He gave me a thumbs up along with a nod of agreement.

Next up for today…. the dreaded call to Mike. I called him, not knowing how he's going to react. Hopefully, he's in an understanding and forgiving mood. I do realize he might be angry with me, and I will deserve it but here it goes….

His phone rang and he was quick to answer. "Hi, Mike, it's me."

"Jenna, where are you?" he asked in a panicked voice. "I've been worried sick about you. We all have." I could hear everyone in the background trying to figure out what's going on.

"Just tell everyone I love them and that I'm buying back our life."

"What are you talking about?" he asked.

"Mike, there's a lot I need to tell you but right now I need to know if Mac is still in Texas."

"As far as I know he is. We haven't heard from him."

"I love you," I told him. "We'll talk soon," and I hung up on him. He tried calling back, but I didn't answer.

I called Mac. No answer. I called again, same. No answer. I quickly became worried. It's not like him to not check in.

I turned to Elmer. "I need to go to the prison where Lola's father is serving his sentence. Mac was supposed to go there, but no one has heard from him, so I don't know if he ever made it. Here's the address," I told him.

"I should probably check in with Patty too," Elmer said.

"Normally, I would agree but not today," I advised. "I don't want to put her in danger. and I'm sure you don't either."

"You're right," he said.

"I'll call my friend Jimmy to go pick her up. Let's just say he's a friend in a position to help. We'll keep her safe," I promised him.

I made the call to Jimmy. He assured me he would go and pick her up asap. "It's going to be okay," I told Elmer "Are you sorry you picked me up yet?" I asked jokingly.

"Not a chance," he replied. "This is the most fun I've had in a long time," he said, laughing.

"Trust me," I told him, "this much excitement is exhausting. You are probably going to hide from me if you see me coming next time."

This time we both laughed.

Chapter Thirteen

We arrived at the prison but missed visiting hours. "I guess we're sleeping in the truck," I announced. "I'm glad we showered at the truck stop and grabbed a bite to eat."

"Me too," he said.

"You can sleep in the back," he said, "and I'll sleep in my driver's seat. It reclines, so I'll be okay."

"Are you sure?" I asked.

"I am, but Ella sleeps back there too."

"No worries," I told him. "My guy Dune sleeps in bed with me too. Ella seems to be okay with me now."

It wasn't long before she decided to curl up with me. *This is so hard*, I thought as I was missing my own dog. I miss Mike and Willow. *Don't do this*, I told myself. *No tears. Keep it together.*

It wasn't long and we were both asleep. Surprisingly, I slept pretty well. I feel so much better now that Mike knows I'm okay.

Just before I fell asleep, I tried calling Mac again, but still no answer. I need to find him. Hopefully, Lola's father can help with that.

I woke at four thirty A.M. Again…there is no way my body says this is a great wake up time. It's just not possible. Elmer was still sleeping. I know this because he also snores. Maybe louder than Mike. I'm convinced, all men snore, and it's apparently louder as they age. Good grief!

I reached up front to the passenger seat and grabbed my backpack. Now is a good a time as any to look through these files. I tried putting them in some kind of order by date. Then I started looking through them for more information.

The first two pages didn't seem to contain anything important. On the third page, the list of names, addresses, and phone numbers had started. There were so many. How can this many people be okay with living a criminal life? I just don't get it. On page four, Junior appeared on the list, confirming what I already knew. He worked for his father. Tears were forming in my eyes. *Turn the page*, I told myself. On the next page was Lola and the men she recruited, and essentially owned. A few were marked "deceased." There must have been forty names on her page. So that must be how they're kept. Each page represents a leader and then the people who work for them underneath.

On page five, I found Bert's name. His name was marked, "Traitor—TBK." Oh my god, TBK? To be killed? Oh, Mac, where are you?

On page six, the list of jobs by employee. I can't look at this anymore. My name will be on one of these lists, making all of this surreal. I put the files back in my bag.

Just then, Elmer woke up. It was almost seven A.M. Visiting hours won't start until nine A.M. "Good morning," I said.

"Good morning to you," he replied.

"Glad you're awake," I told him next. "I have to pee, and I need coffee."

"Well, I guess we need to find coffee and a bathroom. I'm up," he said, moving rather slow.

We didn't have to drive far before finding the amenities we needed. Actually, we found a large truck stop that had showers. We both showered again and got coffee to go. All in one stop. "I feel like a new person," I announced.

"That's good," he said. "You were a bit bossy when I first woke up, I didn't quite recognize you." Then he chuckled.

"Sorry," I told him. "I've actually been awake for a while reading these files. Very disturbing. How was I ever married to such a terrible man? How didn't I see who he was before I married him? I'm so disappointed in myself."

"Don't do this, Jenna. He's not worth your time. In fact, he's not worth a one second of your time. You remember that. Just think about your new life."

"Thank you, Elmer," I said as I gave him a quick kiss on the cheek. "I really am glad I met you."

I think he blushed a little as he changed the subject and started talking about the upcoming prison visit. *What a sweet man*, I thought.

"I don't think you should go in with me," I told Elmer. "I don't want them to know who you are."

"I'm certain we already talked about this. I'm all in," he said. "There's no way they don't already know about me anyway, if everything you told me is true. And I'm certain that it is. Have they picked up my Patty yet?"

"Jimmy assured me they did when I last spoke to him," I said. "I know you don't know me or my family all that well yet, but I promise you they do what they say. In my family, we hug a lot, we eat more than we hug, and we love each other beyond measure. They'll take great care of Patty until you can take over. She is probably having so much fun right now that she hasn't even thought about you at all."

I said that trying not to laugh but I couldn't help myself. Elmer gave me a look of disgust in return and then smiled. "You think you're pretty funny, huh?"

"I can be," I replied, still laughing at his reaction.

"In all seriousness, thank you," he said and then he paused for a second before he finished. Almost like he lost his train of thought.

Then he continued. "I say we get in there and see what we're dealing with. I kinda like to address things head on. I'm a just-get-it-over-with-kind of guy."

I opened my door and said, "I like that. I'm right behind you."

Chapter Fourteen

We entered the prison and went to the front desk of the visitors' section. I told the guard who we were and who we were there to see. The guard gave me a look of concern and then called someone. He told us to take a seat and someone would be out to get us shortly. Elmer and I sat there quietly waiting. Just one look around this place and I was almost freaked out. I cannot imagine being a guard at a prison and having to deal with so many scary people. *I don't have it in me*, I thought.

A few minutes later, they buzzed the door open for us, and a different guard walked us back to the row of glass wall dividers that featured benches on each side. The guard directed us to the end area.

Then we were seated at a window directly across from what appeared to be one of the scariest people I've ever seen. He was a big guy, with dark gray greasy hair pulled up in a ponytail. He had several scars on his face and dark, beady eyes. I'm guessing he was in his late sixties. His tattoos were scary too! It doesn't appear that time has been on his side. He didn't speak, he just glared.

I was terrified but did my best not to show it. Elmer took my hand under the table as I started to speak.

"Hi, I'm Jenna Graham," I said to him in a steady voice.

"I know who you are," he said. "Why are you here?"

"We're looking for your daughter, Lola," I said sternly, trying to be brave. Not sure how well it came across, but he just stared for a moment before answering.

"What makes you think I know where she is? And what makes you think I would tell you if I did? I already told your friend the same thing yesterday."

"Yeah? Was my friend okay when he left here?" I asked. "Do you know where he went?" I knew he was talking about Mac.

"I don't know if any of you are safe," he said rather smugly. "My daughter doesn't listen to her father. She's got a mind of her own. She's a strong, independent woman who makes her own choices. I'm pretty sure she doesn't like you much though," he added.

I sat there for just a minute contemplating my next words, or should we run and get the hell out of there? A tough choice but I'm going with option A, next words.

I looked him straight in the eyes and started to speak. "You know, I've been scared for a long time," I told him. "But the funny thing is, I am no longer scared. I don't know why, but I'm not. I'm not scared of you, and I'm not scared of her, and her opinion of me is none of my concern. It is you and your daughter, however, who should be scared of me. You are protecting your daughter who equally deserves to be where you are. She wanted my worthless husband, so she tried to have me killed. As you can see, that didn't work out so well for her. So now, it's my turn to protect my family. I will do so until there is no longer a surviving reason. Do you understand what I'm saying?"

He continued to look at me in silence, so I continued with what I came to say.

"I have the files proving she was the one who ordered the hit on my life. If she comes near my family or my friends, I'll put a bullet right between her eyes. Then you, too, will learn to live with the loss of a child.

"Furthermore, there's plenty of other information in those files to be shared with every law enforcement agency out there. If you think they're after her now, wait 'til you see what happens when those files are made public. You'll probably need to fear for your own safety too. So I'll ask again, where is she?"

"You're a crazy bitch," he said. "I don't know where she is, but I can get word to her that you need to speak with her."

"You do that," I said as I stood looking down at him like the piece of shit that he is.

"You take care of yourself," I told him turning to leave. He said nothing in return.

We walked out the prison doors, but I felt lots of eyes all over me. I just basically threatened the biggest drug lord in Texas. Oh my god, what was I thinking? My legs are rubber, and I am shaking inside. *I can only hope my fear is not visible*, I thought.

"That was insane," Elmer said as we exited the building. "If I didn't know you, that performance would definitely have me concerned for my own safety. I would say you do have a bit of crazy in you after all. He was rattled, no doubt. Probably making calls as soon as we left."

We got in the truck, and I pulled my gun from my bag and made sure it was loaded and ready to shoot. Just in case whoever is his inside person tries to follow.

"Wow, maybe the semi driver should be more afraid of who he picks up rather than the other way around," Elmer said.

Then we both laughed, but I don't know why. This is no laughing matter, and I know we are both scared to death.

We sat quietly for the next hour. I just kept watching the rear-view mirror. My phone rang and I nearly jumped out of my own skin. "Hello," I said.

"Jenna, it's Mac. Oh, thank goodness you're alive! I've been so worried about you. Where are you? We're going to have a serious talk about you not answering your phone as soon as I see you," I told him.

"Are you okay?" I asked.

"Well, I am now. They just released me," he said.

"What do you mean?" I asked. "Who released you?"

"I was being held in some warehouse. I took a pretty good beating, but I'm good. A few broken ribs, I think."

"Oh Mac, I'm so sorry."

"We need to get off the phone," he said. "Meet me at the place we talked about. The one I gave you to give to Mike. Remember?" Then he hung up.

What place? I was thinking to myself. Then I remembered the paper he gave me. I'm certain he will not be happy when he finds out that I never gave it to Mike. I showed it to Elmer. "How long will it take?" I asked.

"A few hours, tops."

We settled in for the drive ahead. I continued to keep watch while he drove. I kept thinking about the prison visit. I may have been a badass today but what if they only let Mac go to get to me? That's a real possibility. I kept that thought to myself for now.

We were silent for the rest of the drive. My mind was running wild. I couldn't help but wonder what Elmer is thinking about all of this. He doesn't seem to be as scared as I am. I wonder why? Maybe he doesn't get the full grasp of what is really happening or who these people are.

"I don't know what came over me today," I told Elmer. "It's like I'm possessed or something. But the truth is, I'm tired of being afraid. It's either face them or keep running. Keep living in constant fear. Keep worrying about our family. Keep feeling responsible for them and their safety. Keep carrying this unbearable load of guilt. I just can't do it anymore. It's exhausting."

"I bet it is," Elmer agreed. "I hope after all of this is over, you get the closure you're looking for and maybe find peace in all that's happened."

I saw headlights up ahead as we pulled in. I kept my gun close to me just in case it's not Mac. As we got closer, he rolled his window down. It was Mac. A sigh of relief came over me as I jumped out of the truck to greet him. I don't think I've been this happy to see him for a long time. As I hugged him tightly, he winced in pain. "Oh, I'm sorry," I said. "I forgot about your ribs. Are you okay?"

"I will be," he said.

"What happened?" I asked him.

"I'll tell you, but first you tell me how you got here. Please tell me what was so important that you thought you needed to go out on your own? You have a baby to take care of," he said, almost angry. "No one can protect you if you take off on your own. And who is the guy in the truck?"

"Oh, that's Elmer," I said. "He's the truck driver I hitched a ride with." I blurted that out as if hitchhiking is a normal thing people do. "He helped me get here."

"Jesus, Jenna," Mac said in annoyance. "What were you thinking?"

"Well…I was thinking about how I could make things right. I was thinking about how I needed to protect our family. Sorry if you don't like how I went about it." *Now I'm getting angry. I need to calm down*, I was thinking to myself. "And you still haven't answered my question? What happened, how did they capture you?"

I don't think Mac has the strength to deal with me today because he didn't say anything else about me hitching a ride with Elmer. He simply answered my question.

"I talked to Lola's dad at the prison, but he wasn't giving anything up. I was wasting my time, so I left. As I was climbing up in my truck, someone cracked me in the ribs multiple times with a baseball bat. Next thing I knew, I was tied up in a warehouse. I was there for some time, when this guy came and released me. He said some bitch was making demands. Imagine my surprise when I found out it was you," he said, almost annoyed again.

Elmer must have sensed the tension because he climbed out of his truck, walked over, and introduced himself to Mac. He started giving all the details to Mac about the last few days, including all the details about my visit to the prison.

"You really are something," Mac said to me. "I don't even know what to say to you right now."

"How about you thank me for saving your ass," I said. "Does Mike know any of this yet?" I asked.

"Not that I'm aware of, and I'm not telling him…you are." The thought of that doesn't sound pleasant at all.

"Mac, the important thing is that I have all the documents from James's business dealings to include every hit, every murder, and I even got his payroll records. We've got all of them. They're all going to prison for life."

"Does Lola's father know you have this information?" Mac asked.

"He does indeed," I said proudly.

"Shit, Jenna. I'll call Jimmy." While Mac was calling Jimmy to tell him everything, I sat, nervously waiting. Now Jimmy will tell Mike. Mike is going to be so mad at me, or worse, what if he is disappointed in me?

In spite of today, I'm still not sorry. I don't think any one of them could have done what I did today. So I'll deal with Mike when we get home.

Mac hung up and said, "We'll hang here at the warehouse until Jimmy and his guys come and get us.

"Looks like you're coming too, Elmer. Apparently, my mama has taken a liking to your Patty. And until this is over, I'm guessing you'll be staying at the cabin too.

"I don't know how many more of us can fit at the cabin, Mac said, sort of grumbling. "But hey, Mama said bring them home, so they're going home." This time he ended with a heavy sigh.

I just eye-rolled him like I do.

Elmer drove his truck inside the warehouse as Mac instructed. We all sat inside his truck while we waited. The warehouse was black. Being hidden away in here seems like the logical thing to do. Elmer was holding Ella in his lap. Suddenly, I couldn't wait to get home. I'm tired, and I really miss everyone and my puppy.

Chapter Fifteen

I kept waiting all night for some attack to happen. I was sure we were followed. But nothing happened. I heard the helicopter and assumed it was Jimmy. I woke Mac and Elmer. Mac went out first to make sure it was him, and it was, so Elmer and I joined them.

Jimmy gave me a high five and told me, "Nice work." Mac just gave him a look, as if to say *please don't encourage her*. Another eye roll for him I mentally noted. We all climbed up in the helicopter and were in the air in no time. Jimmy said one of his men will drive Elmer's semi back to the cabin. *Great idea*, I was thinking. Just in case his life is in some kind of real danger.

I am definitely a little worried about Mike being mad at me, but…I still can't wait to see him. I can't wait to see Willow and Dune, either. I was feeling excited.

The flight was long, but we finally made it back to the cabin. Just after we landed, Patty came running out to see

Elmer. They hugged for the longest time. I went over and hugged the both of them. I told him I would never have been able to do this without him. He replied by saying, "Somehow I doubt that. Your mind was made up and you were on a mission." I smiled at him and then introduced him to everyone. The entire family came out except for Mike. I'm guessing he's even more mad than I thought. Oh boy.

After the excitement was over, I went looking for him. He wasn't in the house anywhere. But Kristy was holding Willow. I went and kissed my sweet baby and told her I'd be right back.

I went outside and started walking towards the willow tree. I have a feeling I'll find him there.

When I reached the tree, Dune came running out to see me. He was jumping all over me and barking. I picked him up and kissed him, making sure to keep my own mouth closed to prevent a lick to my teeth.

I pulled the branches apart and went in. Mike was sitting on the bench he made to put under the tree. He didn't look at me. I went to sit beside him, and then, softly, I turned his face towards mine. "I'm so sorry, Mike. I didn't mean to hurt you. I was only trying to make things right."

"What exactly does that mean?" he asked.

"It means, I'm tired of the people in this family suffering because of me. Sonja and Mac could possibly lose custody of Susan's boys because of the danger we are all constantly in, Mama is afraid of dying with all of this unresolved, and the list goes on. I don't want our daughter to live in fear for the rest of her life either. I'm done, Mike. I can't do this anymore. So instead of crying like I normally do, I did something about it. I faced Lola's father, and I would do it again. And maybe hitching a ride could have gone sideways, but it didn't. We're all safe, including Mac, because of what I did. And…we gained some friends and family along the way. You don't have to like it, but I hope you'll at least try to understand."

"Well, when you put it like that, it doesn't sound as crazy as it really is," he replied, almost smiling but not quite.

I kissed him and hugged him tight. "I love you, Mike. I have a feeling this is all going to work out."

I asked him to remember the promise we made to each other. "The promise that no problem or situation was bigger than our love for each other. All problems are solvable. We just need to take them to the willow tree to help us remember just how strong our love really is. Nothing can break what we have together. Do you remember?" I asked him.

"I remember," he said. "I've been here a lot over the last few days, praying for your safe return. Just promise me you'll never do that again," he asked. "You put yourself in danger, and I can't live without you. Willow deserves her mother too."

"It was reckless, I know, but we're all okay, and I will never do that again. I promise," I told him.

"Now that you've forgiven me," I said, "we need to get to the house. I want to share what I found at the mansion."

"Okay," he said. I stood and then reached my hands out to him as if to hurry him up. "Come on," I said. "Maybe you can find it in you somewhere to just be proud of me."

"Don't push it, Jenna," he said. I laughed at him and took his hand. We walked back to the cabin at a faster-than-normal pace.

Once inside, the aura was happy. With everyone home safe, things felt almost normal. Mama was cooking with

Patty, the boys were playing a game with Pops, but I could see Elmer sitting back and taking it all in. I can't imagine what he's thinking right now.

"Mike, will you please get Willow from Kristy and bring her back to me? I want you both to meet Elmer. I'm going to go talk to him for a minute until you get there."

"Of course," he agreed and then left to go looking for Kristy.

I walked over to Elmer and gave him a big hug. He hugged me back, saying, "This is some family you have here. I now understand why you had to be crazy for a few days."

I laughed at him. "Well, I wouldn't call me crazy, maybe a bit reckless perhaps," I said.

"No, I'm going with crazy," Mike said, joining our conversation as he was walking back to us with Willow. "I'm still trying to process it all myself." We all laughed as Mike handed Willow to me. "I'm sure you had your hands full with this one," Mike said to Elmer. referencing me.

Elmer replied by saying. "She's hard to keep up with, I'll give you that. But it was the most adventurous trip I've been on in my life." He looked me straight in the eyes and said, "And I would do it all again." I patted his back and smiled. I shifted my focus to Willow as I introduced her to Elmer. He looked at her and said, "She's a beauty," touching her gently on the cheek.

"She's the biggest reason why I had to do what I did. To end all of this madness for all of us, but mostly for her.

"We need to call a family meeting after dinner, adults only," I added. "The children don't need to hear all of the details of what we found." That we all agreed on.

A few minutes later, Mama called dinner. I looked to

Elmer and told him he needed to prepare himself for what was about to happen.

"Why?" he asked in a very serious tone.

"You'll see," I said, laughing as I put my arm in his and led him to the kitchen.

The menu is chicken and noodles, mashed potatoes, peas and carrots, with dinner rolls. Tonight's dessert is a chocolate cake prepared by Patty. It's the recipe she serves in her diner. It all looks amazing, and I cannot wait to eat.

This time the two table leaves were added, making room for our additional guests. Elmer took a seat next to Patty, and they gave each other a very happy look. *How adorable*, I said to myself. *Maybe they need a family too*, I thought.

Anyway, it took a few minutes for everyone to get seated and quiet enough for Pops to say a prayer.

"Dear Heavenly Father, thank you for this meal so graciously prepared for us and our ever-expanding, noisy family."

And then he let out a little laugh as he was saying it. Mama nudged him and then everyone laughed. The ever-expanding, noisy family is a definite truth.

Then Pops continued.

"We have so much to be thankful for today. The safety of our family, the roof over our head, and plenty of love and food to go around. We want to thank you, Lord, for the crossing of paths with those who are meant to be in our lives. Amen."

And then it began. Plates clanking, food flying, and platters being passed, and peas in the floor. I just started laughing as I remembered my first time experiencing a meal with this family. I could see Elmer and Patty looking around. I'm sure they're wondering what the hell are they witnessing right now. I told them, "Go ahead and dig in." It wasn't long and it was like they've known us all forever. *This really is beautiful chaos*, I thought. I love every minute of this. I love every person gathered at our table. My adorable baby girl is sleeping right through it. She's definitely mastered how to tone it all out.

Now, let's add the pack of dogs running through the kitchen, to include Elmer's dog Ella.

Everyone laughed. How could anyone not laugh at the mayhem taking place right now.

I discreetly snapped a few pictures during dinner. Mama didn't say a word if she saw me. But I just want to share these memories with Willow someday. I want her to look at these pictures and not only see the love but feel it.

After dinner, all the girls helped with cleanup. There were a lot of dishes to wash and put away. But that meal was worth every dish we dirtied.

I really want a nap after all that, but the family meeting is much more important.

CHAPTER SIXTEEN

After dinner and clean-up, the kids went to the family room, except for Willow, of course. We made coffee and iced tea and then regrouped at the table.

Sonja and Mac came to sit with Mike and I. Sonja leaned over and whispered, "We're even. I can't believe you, girl."

"I'm so sorry," I told her. "I promise we'll talk about it later." I am certain she wants to discuss me taking off without telling her this time after I scolded her when she did it. And I'll deserve whatever she has to say.

I asked Jimmy to join the family meeting. At this point, he might as well be family. He has been there for us every time we've asked him to be, so I'd say he's earned a spot at our table.

Once we were all seated, and the chatter came to a stop, I pulled the files I took from the mansion out of my bag. Everyone was just watching and waiting. I laid them all out and then started speaking.

"I owe all of you an apology. I am truly sorry for making you all worry. But I did what I thought was best to try and end this constant conflict with the drug cartel. I think I have accomplished that, with the help of my dear friend Elmer," as I gave a nod in his direction.

"I left without a plan, probably not smart, but I just knew I had to fix this problem, and I wasn't going to quit until I did.

"What we have before us," I said, "are all of James's files, to include the attempt on my life, the employees who worked for James, and the hits that were hired out including the one on Mac. We also have information on every drug deal for the last twelve years. We've got everything we need to put them all away."

I continued while everyone remained mostly quiet. "As you've all heard by now, we paid a visit to Lola's father in prison. It was scary no doubt, but I faced him head on. He knows I have every detail about their business. I can honestly say he could have been a bit concerned when I left.

"Mac and Mike, it's up to you to do with this information as you see fit," I further stated.

"We still don't have a location on Lola, but I would guess she's laying low for now if her father has gotten word to her."

Everyone started talking at once. Multiple conversations taking place and I couldn't hear anything.

Mama stood up and shouted, "Hey," to get control. Then she started speaking.

"Look this is fantastic news, for all of us on some level. But on the other hand, you would essentially own them with this information. My thoughts are, they will most definitely come for us. They're not going to sit back and just let us have it. Those documents seal the fate for a lot of people, including Lola and her father.

"Mike? Mac? What are your thoughts?" Mama asked?

"Well, initially, my thoughts did not go there, but it's a valid point," Mac agreed, "so we need to continue being on high alert." Jimmy agreed as well.

"So, you think all I did was stir up a hornets' nest?"

"No, I'm not saying that," Mama said. "I do think stirring the hornets' nest is a good thing, I just don't know if we're prepared for what's to come. For all we know, the master plan is to get us all together again, kill two birds with one stone so to speak."

"Jimmy, how fast can you mobilize your teams and move us to another location?" Mac asked.

"Mid-morning at best," he replied. "We'll need at least three choppers this time, if not four."

"I'm not even sure it's possible with many people to be honest," Jimmy stated.

The chatter started all at once again.

"Everyone, please!" I hollered. "Look, you all have an opinion but so do I. I say we move the children to a secure location, and those who want to stay should stay, those who want to go with the children should go. I don't want to run for the rest of my life. I can't speak for any of you, but I'm speaking now for me and my daughter. I'm staying. I will no longer run and live in fear. This has to end."

Mike came and stood beside me. "I'm staying too."

One by one, everyone decided to stay, finally agreeing to move the children.

"Now that we've settled on staying," Mac said, "I say we call in all the manpower we can get. If there's going to be a war this time, we need soldiers, and a lot of them."

"Agreed," Mike said. Not a minute later, Mike, Mac, and

Jimmy were all on the phone making calls to various people. It's happening. They're calling in the calvary.

A few hours later, which was around midnight, everyone said good night and headed to their rooms.

Once inside our room and alone, I thanked Mike for standing with me on the decision to stay. "I really think it's the right thing to do."

"You're my wife, I'll always stand with you," he replied. "But after hearing everyone else's thoughts, I am in agreement with your assessment. She'll make her way here no doubt. I just hope we're prepared to take them on."

"Me too. I don't need another suggestion that I made come back and cause further trauma to the family."

"It won't," Mike assured me.

We showered and went to bed. Unfortunately, sleep did not come easy again tonight. My brain could not stop thinking about recent events. I hope Mama is not upset that I openly disagreed with her. But I keep telling myself it's okay to see a situation differently than how someone else may see it.

And then there's Mike next to me snoring...very loud! *I'm not finding it comforting tonight at all*, I thought. Ugh! A very long night ahead of me or… I could get the dinner bell out that I bought for Mama and give it a jingle right in his ear. I pictured that in my head for a moment as I laughed out loud at myself. Maybe next time. I'm sure there will be many, many more nights of snoring for a next time.

I turned to look at him and watched him sleep. Aside from his snore problem, he's actually pretty perfect. Funny how we learn to accept things about the people we love.

What is okay with one person, may not be with another. I wonder if he thinks that about me sometimes. I mean, I came with a lot of baggage. Yet he seems to be tolerant and accepting of me in every aspect. In the big scheme of things, it almost seems like a miracle that two people ever find each other and make it work. I guess there really is something bigger than us that helps us find our way to where we're meant to be.

My thoughts were beginning to fade as I finally drifted off to sleep.

Chapter Seventeen

I awoke to lots of noise outside. Mike was gone, and so was Willow. Dune was right beside me, of course. He jumped up and pounced on me. I carefully protected my mouth from his very active tongue.

We got up and headed to the kitchen. "Apparently, I overslept," I said when I saw everyone in the kitchen. Jimmy was doing his thing. He brought a helicopter to take the kids to a safe location. Mike handed Willow to Kristy. "Wait," I said to Mike, "let me hold her for just a moment," as tears filled my eyes. "This is not what I expected to wake up to," I told him.

"I know," he said, touching my hand briefly, "but things are happening fast. I'll fill you in after the helicopter takes off.

"Kristy is going to go with them," he said, "so she can stay with the children. I think it's best since Willow is very comfortable with her. And I thought you would agree."

"That's an excellent idea," I said, "and I do feel better having your sister care for her." I handed Willow back to Kristy after I kissed her tiny face several times. It wasn't long and it was up in the air with my baby, heading to who knows where. I couldn't stop the tears, but I know she's in capable hands. I'm always second-guessing myself when it comes to Willow. I just don't want to make any mistakes with her like I did with Junior. My choices and decisions need to be solid.

Mike put his arm around my shoulder as we watched the helicopter until it was no longer visible. Then he turned to me and said, "We're doing the right thing."

"Are you trying to convince me or yourself?" I asked.

"Both, I think," he said in response.

We headed back to the house and gathered at the table to discuss updates and next steps. It was so quiet without the kids. *Everyone must be thinking the same thing*, I thought as I looked around at their faces. *Lord, please let this happen fast so we can get on with our lives.*

Mac started with his update, telling everyone that the DEA is going to assist the FBI, allowing the FBI to take the lead on the apprehension of Lola. He further added that with the information provided in James's files, they have enough to start making arrests. And there are many arrests to be made; it's going to take some time.

Mike chimed in. "As far as we know, Lola hasn't had any direct contact with her father in prison, but we still don't know who her inside man is. She could be communicating with her father through someone else. We're still working that angle. The FBI has an agent going through prison camera footage now. Hopefully, we'll get an update soon.

"So for now, we hang tight and hope she comes to us. If we thought she was mad before, we can expect her anger to intensify greatly. We've gone after her real family, and now we're going after her work family. She won't sit tight, and she won't ever turn herself in."

One of the guards had a few things to add. "Hey, everyone. I know you've seen me around but I'm Adam. There is a group of FBI agents coming in tonight, actually around two A.M. It will hopefully be more discreet for them during those hours. When they arrive, please stay in your rooms like nothing is going on. We want the house to remain dark during this time. That's all for now," he said.

I could see Mama just shaking her head. I know she's concerned. What mama wouldn't be? I went and stood beside her. "I'm sorry, Mama."

"I know you are," she replied. "I'm just worried, as you already know. They've had lots of cases through the years, but this one scares me for some reason. It's just too close to home. Too personal."

"Please don't say that, Mama," I said. "Everyone knows when you have a feeling it's always right." She just reached for my hand and held it.

Mama must be way more nervous than I thought. She's not even making breakfast. Maybe I should make breakfast. I went and looked for Sonja. She left the family meeting early.

I found her on the porch. "Hey," I said to her.

"Hey back," she said.

"Are you okay?" I asked.

"Not really, you?"

"I'm not okay either," I told her. "But we will be one day, I just know it."

"You know, this is the reason I didn't want a DEA husband. I don't want to grieve the loss of him. Every time he puts himself in danger, I have to worry he might not come home. I love him more than I have ever loved anyone, and that makes it unbearable."

"I understand what you're saying, Sonja, but you can't run from love because they could get hurt or die. I realized that myself when I practically demanded that Mike leave the FBI. I saw what it was doing to him. It's just not fair to them. We both knew what they did for a living when we entered a relationship with them. Whether you told him you wouldn't marry him until he got out or not, you still stayed in a relationship with him for the better part of eight years."

"You're right," she said, "but every time he gets shot, I get a glimpse of what could happen and the realization that he could die."

"True, but should something happen to either one of them, we can be thankful for the time we did have together. I know, for me, there is nobody else I want to spend my life with, so I have to accept that part of him."

"You're right," she said again. "Where is Mac, anyway? she asked.

"When I was on my way out to find you, they were heading for the tunnel," I replied. "Planning our defense strategy, I'm sure." . She just rolled her eyes.

"I actually came to find you and see if you wanted to help me cook some breakfast. The crew needs to eat, and Mama isn't feeling it today."

"Yeah, sure," Sonja agreed, "but cooking isn't my thing."

"I know but I thought it could get our minds off of all of this for a while," I told her.

We got up and headed to the kitchen. We ended up making a jumbo pot of oatmeal, with cranberries, walnuts, brown sugar, butter, and cinnamon. We made toast and ham on the side. It turned out amazing.

After breakfast, we cleaned up and headed to the living room. Mama and Pops must have headed to take a nap, although it's early for them. Elmer and Patty aren't here either. It seems so weird to not have Willow here with me. Everything just feels off.

That said, I need to find something to do to get my mind off of all of this. I grabbed my journal and pen and threw them in my bag. I decided I'm going to face my fears and go to the cottage. I haven't gone back since Mama shot and killed James there. However, I have this fearless, independent thing still going on as of late, so I would say it's a good time to go and see if I actually have the courage.

I headed out towards the cottage. It's a beautiful, sunny afternoon. I passed the tunnel but couldn't hear the guys. I kept walking and passed the willow tree. I almost went in but decided I would stay the course and face my fears at the cottage.

As I neared the cottage, I could hear someone talking inside. I ducked out of window-view and tried to listen. My heart once again racing as I was thinking this was a bad idea. But someone is in our cottage. I reached into my bag and pulled out my gun. I'm going in. *I really have lost my mind*, I'm thinking to myself. I promised Mike no more reckless decisions, but how do I just walk away?

I bravely peeked in through the tiny window, hoping no one saw me. I could see Mama, Pops, Elmer, and Patty tied up in chairs. Oh my god! I found my phone and called Mike, no answer. Then I tried Mac, no answer. My hands are shaking. I really have no choice. I decided, putting my hand on the door handle as I said a prayer and pushed it open. I had my gun pointed straight ahead.

I didn't see anyone else at the moment, so I quickly went to untie Mama. The look on her face told me someone was behind me. I turned and, sure enough, there was a guy rushing towards me. I shot him in the ankle. He wailed in pain and dropped to the floor. I continued towards Mama, this time keeping my back towards her until I was close enough to untie her. All the while keeping my eyes on the guy I shot. He was rolling around, moaning and grunting. I told him to shut up or he'd take another one to his other ankle. He just looked at me as if he'd seen a monster. Once Mama was loose, she started to untie the others.

I looked at the injured guy and asked him, "How many more of you are here?" He just looked at me without saying a word. "Last chance," I said, pointing my gun at him.

He didn't answer, so I shot him again in the other ankle, at least making sure he's not going anywhere. He let out a horrible scream. I almost felt guilty and then I quickly came to reason. He's in our house uninvited and tied up my family. He's lucky I let him live.

Once everyone was untied, we left the cottage. I tried calling Mike again; no answer. Now I know something is wrong.

Mama thanked me for coming to their rescue. "How did this happen?" I asked her.

"We were giving Elmer and Patty a tour of the property," she said. "But how did you know we were here?" Mama asked.

"I didn't. I decided that I was going to the cottage to write and face my fears. I could see you all tied up through the window. And I heard voices I didn't recognize," I said, "so I knew I had to come in."

Elmer said, "I told you that you would figure things out without me."

"Yes," Mama said. "You've really gotten strong and independent. I'm proud of you."

"Thanks, Mama." We headed towards the tunnel, creeping around like we don't own this place. *This is wrong on so many levels*, I thought.

Once there, we went in, but no one was there. I don't understand where they could be. "Let's get back to the cabin," I told everyone. I could hear gunfire in the distance. *Where are the FBI agents?* I was thinking to myself.

"We need weapons," I told Mama. "Pops, I need you to call 911."

We approached the cottage from the side. Mama said, "If we can get to the back door, we can get to the basement. I have a few guns there."

"Let's go," I said, trying to keep them all safe. I let Mama lead as I followed close behind, keeping my gun pointed.

We got to the back door and there was a guard there. Not an FBI agent. Not one of us. He drew his weapon and Pops smacked him in the head with a brick he picked up from the patio. I didn't even see him grab it. Pops said, "If you would have shot him, then Lola's men would have heard it. In turn bringing unwanted attention to us."

"Good call," I told him.

Mama was able to get to the basement and get what

weapons she needed. She handed the others a small gun and kept the shotgun for herself.

We entered the main part of the cabin. It was silent. "I don't understand, where is everyone?" I asked.

"They're here," Mama said. Just then, there was a loud explosion. "Oh my god!" Mama cried. "The tunnel! Mike and Mac were out there earlier!"

I felt numb but remained calm. I don't know why or how, but I guess it's better than hysteria. The elders started running to the tunnel. I just walked and maintained my composure. *There's no need to fall apart now,* I told myself.

As we neared the tunnel, Jimmy was lying in the grass, no pulse. He was gone. He appeared to have been shot in the chest. Mama and I both started crying.

There was still a small opening at the tunnel entrance, but not big enough to get out. I started calling out for Mike and Mac. I could hear mumbling from behind the rubble.

We started moving debris to try and get to them. Finally, after what seems like forever, there are sirens in the distance. Help is on the way. Thank God they're almost here.

I pulled Mama aside. "I need to go back to the cabin," I told her. "I heard voices, so that means someone else was in there. For all I know, it's Lola. I can't let her get away again."

Mama nodded and touched my cheek softly. "Stay safe." she said. I gave her a nod and then turned to leave.

I headed back to the cottage. I ran about half the way until I couldn't run anymore. I'm exhausted. And now it's starting to get dark. I checked my hip and made sure my knife was still there. I reloaded my gun and opened the door.

There she was, sitting in the chair. Almost like she was expecting me.

"I heard you were looking for me," she said.

I kept my gun pointed at her. A guy came up from behind and put his arm around my neck in a chokehold. I used my right arm and pulled my knife and stabbed him in the groin. His blood was gushing. I hit an artery. I quickly turned back to Lola and could see her disbelief, but she didn't speak or react.

"You heard right. I recognize him," I told her. "The guard from the prison. Your new boyfriend?" I asked sarcastically. "He's the one who helped you escape?"

"And your point?" she asked?

"No point. Just clarifying the roles here."

"You've changed," she sneered.

"More than you know," I said. "Why are you here?" You had a great place reserved especially for you in a prison cell. You didn't like your accommodations?"

"I think I liked the old you better," Lola stated.

"Sorry to disappoint you," I said. "I'm sure we could go back and forth with this all day but I've got better things to do right now. I'm going to need you to take a walk with me. Get up," I told her.

"I'm not interested in a walk," she said.

"Too bad. Get up, Lola. I know you were in here earlier, so you know I won't hesitate to shoot you. I'll say it one more time. Get. Up."

Again, she sat there. A million things are running through my mind right now. If I don't end this, she will keep coming for me.

In the few seconds I took to process the situation, she fired a shot that hit me in the shoulder. I fell back into the wall, but I was still holding my gun. I could see her walking closer. I raised the gun with my good arm and fired back. As she was falling, I fired again, this time shooting her in the chest. Out of breath, I mumbled, "You lose, Lola."

I remember slouching to my side and trying to hold my wound, but I couldn't stay awake….

My last thought before surrendering to darkness was, *I am going to die, but my baby girl is safe*. I could let go.

Chapter Eighteen

I don't know what happened next. I was coming to for brief periods of time. I could hear a paramedic talking to me, but his words made no sense. Nothing made sense.

I remember trying to tell him about the explosion, but I don't know if I was making any sense to him either.

I woke up two days later in the hospital. Mike was sitting in the chair beside me. It was so bright in the room that I could barely see. Mike was calling for the nurse. "Hey there," he said to me. "You gave us all a pretty good scare."

My mouth was so dry that when I spoke, it sounded hoarse. "Where's Willow?" is all I could get out.

"At the cabin, with the family," Mike replied. "She's safe, we're all safe."

"I don't understand, where were you?" I asked. "I kept calling, but no one answered.

Jimmy's dead," I sobbed.

"I know, sweetheart, and I'll tell you everything, but right now you need to rest."

A minute later, there were doctors and nurses in my room. Everyone was asking me lots of questions, taking my blood pressure and checking my shoulder.

I could see Mike stepping out of the room. Next, I could hear him talking on the phone, but I couldn't make out his words. I'm just so tired. I fell back asleep before getting to talk further with Mike.

The next morning when I woke again, Mike was still there. "Good morning," I said to him.

"Good morning," he said back to me. He got up and walked closer. "You really scared me. I thought I was going to lose you," he said as his eyes filled with tears.

"I'm so sorry, Mike. I have no idea what's come over me. I feel invincible sometimes. And sometimes I feel like it's on me to resolve everything for the family. After all, this all started because of me," my eyes also filling with tears.

We just held each other for a few minutes as the tears were falling. Then Mike started to speak. "It's over this time. You did it. Your craziness actually took down the largest cartel in the US. You took down Lola, her dad, and basically their whole organization."

"Her dad?" I said, puzzled.

"Someone stabbed him. We don't know who, but I don't think anyone will try to figure it out, either."

I cried some more. Those words "it's over" were the very words that I have been waiting to hear for so long. Mike and I held our hands and heads tightly together, almost as if we were praying. And maybe we were.

There was a knock on my door. It was Mac and Sonja

with my baby girl. The tears kept coming. I'm an emotional mess right now.

I held her as best I could, but it was difficult with one arm. After a few minutes, Mike took her from me.

Mac had a wrap on his ribs to help them heal. "I'm so sorry about Jimmy," I told him. "I know you two were friends for a really long time."

"Yeah, I'm sorry too," Mac said. "He and I have been through and seen a lot of shit together. He will be a missing piece of my life forever." We were all sort of sobbing at that point.

Then Mama and Pops came in. Lots more hugs. Lots more tears.

Mama told me they won't allow any more visitors, so I won't be able see the rest of the family until I get home.

"I want to go home," I announced to everyone.

"I think you can go home tomorrow," Mike said.

"I am ready to hear what happened."

"Are you sure?" Mike asked.

"I am," I replied.

Mike started to fill me in. Someone called in a tip about Lola's location to the FBI Hotline. The tip said Lola and her men were spotted near the mansion. Everyone assumed she was going there to hide out for a little while. So, the FBI agents watching the cabin left to help with her apprehension. Turns out, the tip was called in by the prison guard who helped her to escape. They were already on their way before they realized it wasn't a valid tip.

"Mac, Mark, and I were in the tunnel, but near the back, so there's no phone reception.

"Jimmy was outside the tunnel entrance keeping watch. They must have come up on him before he even realized it.

"We heard the blast and took cover until the debris settled. The opening was blocked with the exception of one small hole. With Mac's broken ribs, he couldn't help us move debris to get us out.

"While Mama, Pops, Elmer and Patty, were trying to help from the other side, it was pretty much useless. The fire department arrived and helped us get out several hours later.

"Mama told the search team that you were at the cottage. Once they found you, you were life-flighted to the hospital. You had lost a lot of blood and weren't conscious.

"The police came and then later the FBI arrived. Since then, the FBI has been making arrests. The story made the headlines. You're a hero. A few news channels have reached out for your statement."

I looked around the room at all of them. "I…I don't know what to say. I did what I had to do to protect our family from some really bad people. I don't think I want to talk about it to anyone. I just want to be free."

Mike came and put his head to mine and said, "You are free. It really is over." He kissed me softly on my cheek.

I was suddenly feeling very tired. The nurse came in and told everyone to leave except Mike. "Wait," I said. "Mama, do you think you could make pancakes when I get home tomorrow?"

Everyone laughed, and Mama nodded her head as if she were happy my first meal request was her pancakes. They all left, and it was just Mike and I. They brought me some dinner, to include chicken noodle soup, crackers, applesauce, and a Jell-O cup. I struggled to eat it because my mind is set on pancakes. However, this is my first meal in several days. I'll try to choke it down. *I hope tomorrow comes fast*, is all I kept thinking.

CHAPTER NINETEEN

I'm finally going home today. I was sitting up in the hospital bed, dressed in my own clothes, waiting on the doctor to sign my discharge paperwork. "I'm losing my patience by the minute," I told Mike. "I'm serious. I want to go home."

"I know you do but this is the process. And you really need to work on your patience. You're just mad because you want pancakes," he added in a sarcastic voice. I looked over to him and smiled because I knew he was right.

It wasn't too much longer before they came and talked to me. They went over my wound care, get lots of rest…and blah blah blah. I stopped listening when they got to the diet part. *I'm having pancakes so that part doesn't matter much anyway*, I thought. They helped me into the wheelchair and wheeled me out the door. There were reporters everywhere. I thought it best to just give them something quick so they would leave us alone.

In my statement, I simply repeated what I said to the family earlier. "I did what I had to do to protect our family.

The decision was easy for me. That's all I have. I am going to ask that you all respect our privacy while we heal and mourn the loss of our dear friend Jimmy. Thank you."

"One last question please," asked one of the reporters.

"Yes?" I answered.

"What's next for you personally? Now that this is all over?"

"I'm going to heal physically, I'm going to raise my daughter with my husband, and I'm going to open a women's shelter for abused women. We're taking donations to help get it started," I added. "We need clothes, shoes, linens, and personal care items."

"That's all for today. Thank you."

I turned to Mike, "Take me home, please," I asked. He helped me climb into his truck and we pulled away. We were quiet for a few minutes and then he asked if I was okay. "I am," I told him. "I am better than okay," I said, smiling.

"Do you need to talk to anyone after the shootings? Maybe a counselor of sorts?"

"No, I don't believe I do. I feel it was justified to save my own life and the lives of our family. I'll never have any regrets. The only decisions I'll ever make now will be decisions that make me proud. I'm looking forward from here on out. I will never look back."

I asked Mike to stop at the bookstore before heading home. "I'm looking for something specific," I told him. "A book about willow trees. I want it for the journal I'm working on."

"Okay," he said.

We stopped at the bookstore and Mike ran in to get the book I asked for, and then we headed home.

Once we arrived, it seemed quiet, peaceful, I thought as I looked around. I opened the front door, and that thought was quickly abandoned. "SURPRISE!"

They had welcome home signs, balloons, and a beautiful cake with sprinkles. Dune was jumping all over me. I reached down to pet him.

Mama helped me to the kitchen and then told me that the cake was literally stacked pancakes. "It is beautiful," I told her. Almost too pretty to eat but I was going to eat it anyway. "I'm so hungry," I said, smiling. I cut the pancakes as if they were a real cake. I put butter and maple syrup all over them, and then sprinkled on homemade bacon bits on the top. "Oh my goodness, I've missed these." We all laughed, and the chaos resumed.

I saw Elmer and Patty standing in the corner, looking around at everyone. I waved for them to come join me.

"I'm so happy you're still here," I told them both.

"Mama asked us to stay," Patty said, "but I have a diner to run. We'll be leaving to head home soon. I need to reopen the diner before my customers forget about us," she said, smiling but sad at the same time.

"Promise me you'll stay in touch," I said with tear-filled eyes. I gave them both a hug and asked them to sit with me while we ate. They were happy to do so.

Elmer announced that he and Patty are finally going to get married.

"I'm so excited for both of you! I think you should get married here at the cabin."

Mama was apparently listening and then shouted across the room that she thought that was a great idea. "I'll call you to work out the details."

"How in the world did she hear our conversation over all this mayhem?" Elmer asked. "And from the other end of the room!"

We laughed as I shared the rumor about Mama hearing EVERYTHING! "I guess it's true," I said as I winked at Mama.

I took a pause and looked around the room to the people I loved so much and could no longer live without. I don't know what happens now, but I hope somehow we can all still stay together. I looked to Mike who was holding Willow and gave him a big smile. I whispered, "I am home. I am happy." He simply smiled back at me.

After brunch, I asked Mike to grab my bag. I told him I had something special for Mama. A souvenir to remember me by. Everyone got quiet while we waited for Mike to return. He handed me my bag. I started digging through it until finally I found it at the bottom. I handed it to Mama, telling her that this was a special handmade gift. Then I apologized for all the times she waited on this large group for dinner because we couldn't get word to everyone at the same time. "There will be no excuse for late dinner arrivals going forward," I stated, handing the wrapped package to Mama.

She seemed surprised by my gesture as she took the package from my hand. You could hear a pin drop as all eyes were on Mama. Her frail, aging hands struggled to remove the tape. Mike reached over to help. She held the bell after the packaging was removed and began to weep. To recover from the emotion, she simply asked why no one had ever thought to get her one in all these years. Then she hugged me and told me she loved it.

After the dishes were washed and put away, we all headed to the family room. Me, Mike, Willow, and Dune, of course, took our big, round chair. I attempted to cover myself with a blanket, but Mike had to help.

Mac and Sonja took the couch with loungers. Mac was holding his dog as well as Jimmy's dog. Mac and Sonja decided they are going to keep him. Both dogs were just lying there being well behaved.

Not our dog Dune. He was rolling all over Mike and dropping his ball in his lap. Apparently, he doesn't need a nap. I scooped him up with my good arm to get him to settle down.

It wasn't long, and we were all asleep. It's been an exhausting month for everyone.

Chapter Twenty

Three weeks later...

Mac and I are both practically healed and feeling pretty good. Everyone is still staying at the cabin even though we no longer really need to, except Elmer and Patty. I can't say for sure why none of us have left. Maybe there is some lingering doubt about our safety...

I personally haven't left the cabin since the shooting, but I am feeling ready to get out and about. I asked Mike to drive me to the diner to see Elmer and Patty. That will take the better part of the day, but I miss them, so it's worth the two-hour drive there to see them. I've talked to them on the phone, but I want to visit them in person. I told Mike I needed to change my clothes and that I would meet him out front in a few minutes.

After I changed my clothes, I grabbed the bag of money that we found in the bedpost and then headed outside. Mike was already in the truck but got out to open my door.

"What do you have there?" he asked, referring to the bag in my hand.

"It's the bag of money I found hidden in the bedframe at the mansion. After everything Elmer did for me, I want him to have it. He wouldn't take it before, but I'm going to ask him to reconsider."

"Oh, okay," he said, hopping back in the driver's seat. We backed out and started heading down the long winding driveway.

We were mostly quiet as we took in the beauty all around us. This land is virtually untouched. The tall grass was dancing in the wind, the river flowing steady, and the sun was warm and bright. I kept my face towards the sun so I could feel its warmth. "I will never get tired of seeing this beautiful place," I said in a faint voice, but loud enough for Mike to hear. He stayed silent but reached over to touch my hand. He watched me as I looked around in awe. *There are so many incredible places to be seen*, I thought to myself. I know I haven't begun to imagine all the beauty that exists, but I can finally look forward to experiencing it. It will be so exciting to share these new places with my daughter and Mike. So many memories to make and look forward to. The long-awaited peace that I am experiencing right now could not feel any more amazing. Even in my dreams, I did not imagine this. I will remember this feeling for as long as I live without a doubt.

It didn't seem like two hours had passed, but we arrived at the diner and went in. Patty was behind the counter, taking orders like before, and Elmer was sitting at the counter on the patron side. He's no longer driving a semi, so he spends a lot of time at the diner.

"I'm so happy to see you," I told the both of them. We all hugged and exchanged hellos. Once we were seated at the counter, Mike and I ordered some lunch, to include her famous coconut cream pie. I can see why people come here just to have a slice of this incredible dessert. I ordered a whole one to go so we could share with the family.

After we ate, I asked if she and Elmer had a minute to go in the back to talk. "Of course," they both agreed. I pulled out the bag of money. I started to talk about how I wanted them to have it. Elmer began pushing the bag back to me.

"Honey," he said, "we don't need your money, we're financially okay. We can't take it. And you don't owe us anything."

"Okay, but you said you would take a cut when we found it," I told Elmer.

"My cut can go towards your women's shelter. Maybe you can even name it after me," he said with a huge smile. "That can be my contribution to help start it, anyway."

"Okay," I told him. "I would be honored to name it after you." I hugged them both goodbye and slipped a few bundles of money in Patty's apron pocket. I whispered in her ear, "Please take this for a rainy day." She hugged me and then quietly thanked me. We giggled like two schoolgirls with a big secret. I told them we'd be back for a visit soon and that they were always welcome at the cabin.

"Same here. You will always have a seat in my diner," Patty replied.

After one last hug, we said our final goodbyes. Mike and I left and headed back to the cabin. On the way back, he said, "That was a very sweet thing you did today. I'm proud of you. I'm even more proud that you have never wavered on being a good person. With all the bad you have endured, you prevailed at life, at love, and at all that you do. Thank you for choosing me to spend your life with. I'm all in on the women's shelter," he added. "We'll make it happen, I promise."

"Thank you for that. It means a lot to me."

"I know," he said in return.

"Do you think we'll stay in touch with Elmer and Patty?" I asked Mike.

"I do," he said. "I really like them both. We probably would have never met them if it weren't for the stunt you pulled." Then he smiled.

"I know you're right," I told him, "but are you going to keep reminding me of my temporary insanity situation? Although, it is funny how that all worked out. I feel like I have known them for years."

"Yes, it does," he agreed.

We were silent for the rest of the drive home, just like on the way there. I'm sure we are both thinking about the last few weeks. I know I am, anyway. Riding in the truck with him is my Zen place. My place to ponder, dream, and process. Maybe it's his too. Either way, I love our time together while we drive.

Once we arrived at the cabin, we spent some time with Willow. After she fell asleep, I ran a hot lavender bubble bath and pulled my hair up. I grabbed the book Mike bought for me about willow trees and finally started reading it. I couldn't put it down. I read the entire book, which was well over a hundred pages. My bath water was now very cold, and I was freezing. I dried off quickly threw on my panties and a sweatshirt, then crawled into bed. I didn't even know what time it was. Mike was already asleep. I moved in close to steal his body heat. He didn't seem to mind.

I lay there in the dark for what felt like hours before finally falling asleep myself. Unfortunately, it wasn't for long. My mind is restless and apparently doesn't shut down even for sleep. So now that I'm awake… again, I just lay there in the dark, thinking about the last year of my life, and thinking about the weeping willow tree. Mike and I both love the willow tree for many reasons, but it wasn't until this very moment that I actually understood the significance of the willow tree and its similarities as it relates to my life.

The willow tree itself is described as a large tree, with long, flowing branches. The leaves of the willow tree often symbolize flexibility and adaptability, while the limber nature of its extremities means it bends to accommodate and withstand strong winds and adverse weather.

The leaves represent the balance, harmony, and the growth we experience through the storms of life challenges. The willow tree gives us hope, a sense of belonging and safety. Additionally, giving us the ability to let go of the pain and suffering to grow new, strong, and bold.

I now understand my life as it relates to the willow tree. I too, have endured and survived so many things. This last year has given me the courage and strength to move forward and let go of my past. In turn, I have gained a family that loves and protects each other. I have emerged a strong and confident woman who is able to freely love and cherish every moment of this beautiful life.

This gift of living that we are given may not always be perfect, and the choices we make determine the next path for each of us. Every new choice can alter or change the current life direction. If we're true to ourselves through each life choice, we can be assured we are living the life we are meant to live.

Suddenly, I had chills that could not be explained. I knew at that very moment I am right where I am supposed to be. My life now has meaning far beyond my own understanding.

The weeping willow tree, as it relates to my life, represents everything I hold dear to me. With so much to be thankful for, my past can now be put to rest.

I turned to look at Mike with deep adoration, but he was awake and watching me too. "What are you thinking about?" he asked.

"So many things," I replied. "Meet me at willow tree tomorrow afternoon and I'll share everything about my new realization.

"Thank you for loving me," I told him. "My life is amazing, far more than I could have ever imagined for myself. I'm so afraid I'll wake up and it will all have been a beautiful dream. Some sort of glimpse of a life that doesn't really belong to me."

"It's real," he said, "and this life does belong to you, to us." Then he leaned over and kissed me with a hunger that I, too, was feeling. "I can't wait to meet you at the willow tree," he said with a grin. "Can we move that meeting to the morning instead of afternoon?" he asked.

I laughed quietly and then whispered, "I'm the luckiest woman in the world," as we drifted off to sleep.

The End